For My Son

by Robert Young

Copyright 1998

All rights reserved. No part of this book
may be reproduced without written
permission from the author or the publisher.

Winnipeg Free Press and Winnipeg Sun Articles reprinted
with permission

One Man's Opinion, Peter Warren CJOB,
courtesy of Manitoba Blue Cross

ISBN 0-9685114-0-6

Printed by Hignell Printing Limited, Winnipeg, Canada

Cover designed by
Ron Able Media Services

Edited by
J. Knight
M. Vaccaro
D. Lesage
N. Vadas

Acknowledgments

I'd like to take this opportunity to thank and acknowledge all those who were there when I needed you most. Your sympathy, kindness, guidance and strength will be something I will carry with me for the rest of my life. Dave (Gouch) Guttman, Debbie & Jerry Lesage, Melanie (I hope it's spelled right) Verhaeghe, Kristen Firth, Gerald Fast, Peter Warren, Michelle, Jake & Aaron (you guys are the best) Pearcey, Mrs. P, Sharon S, Abe Rennie, Tania, Jen and the rest of the girls, Susan Thompson, Sharon Wolfe, Ron Able, Hal Anderson, John & Janice Angus, Ward & Caroline, Mom & Dad, Tim & Helen, Carolyn & George, Jaylene Knight, Michelle Vaccaro, Kevin Conner, Brad & Heather Penno, Terri & Don Bell, Garry & Judy Fitch, Mark & Val, Garth Steek, Karen Huttman, Frank Kowalski, Shane & Janet, Harry L., Gordon Sinclair, Deano, Krystal, Megan & her Mom, Kim, Jack & Peggy, Kelly, Kevin & Marc, and anyone else I may have forgotten. Your thoughts and prayers were my strength, your smiles and your touch were my encouragement. Thank you all.

To laugh often and much,
to win the respect of intelligent people
and the affection of children,
to learn the appreciation of honest critics
and endure the betrayal of false friends,
to appreciate beauty,
to find the best in others,
to leave the world a bit better,
whether by a healthy child,
a garden patch or a redeemed social condition,
to know even one life has breathed easier
because you lived.
This is to have succeeded

1

April 23, 1997
Why? A Father's Grief
by Gordon Sinclair
Winnipeg Free Press

More than three hours after his 14 year old boy was swallowed by a swirling culvert intake pipe, his father was trying to explain what kind of kid Adam Young was.

"He was out sandbagging this weekend," Rob Young said, trying to control the sobbing. "Helping out people."

The details of the Garden City drowning yesterday at noon remain as murky as the ditch water that swept him into the city's sewer system.

Late yesterday afternoon, minutes before firefighters abandoned the search at Leila Avenue and Manila Road - within screaming distance of the boy's school, Leila North, Rob Young was asking reporters for details.

What's known is a small group of middle students,

who had left school after lunch were gathered near the ditch in front of the school.

Two boys - one of whom was chasing something in the thigh-high run off water - were sucked into a two foot wide water-covered intake pipe that acted like an unplugged bathtub. The manhole cover or grate was missing from the pipe.

Firefighters whose station is right beside the culvert were alerted and managed to save the younger boy.

According to what police told Rob Young, Adam was trying to rescue the other boy, who is 11.

Why the pipe was open is a question Young was asking late yesterday afternoon. But no one had an answer.

I'm reading it, but it's not sinking in. I'm sitting in a coffee shop. It's 4:30 in the morning and it just won't sink in. This is my son he's written about. Adam, my first born.

There's more to this story than what's printed in the papers and being read on the news. It's all their talking about. The two guys at the next table are talking about Adam.

Why won't it sink in?

I know it's happened, but somehow it doesn't seem real. It's not a dream It can't be my son. Not Adam. Like cancer, it has to be happening to someone else.

It's been 16 hours since I received the call on my cell phone. It's kind of ironic, I was sitting in the same coffee shop only 15 minutes away from where the accident happened.

I was on my way to take Adam and Kevin (my middle son) to lunch as a surprise, but realized that I would never make it on time. So I was just killing time having a coffee.

I remember thinking how surprised they would be when if I showed up just before lunch and took them out for a burger. If only I had, everything would be different.

That phone call is something that's going to remain with me for a long time.

"Mr. Young, this is the Winnipeg Police. We need you to come to the Fire Hall on Leila and Manila. There's been an accident," the voice said.

"What happened," I asked.

"Mr. Young we need you to come here as soon as you can. Do you need a ride? I can have someone pick you up. Where are you?"

"What's going on? I'm ten minutes away," I said.

"Please drop what you're doing and get here."

That's all they would say. I can't remember how many different scenarios went through my head in that short time. Who was it? What happened?

As I approached the scene, all I could see were police cars and people.

People were standing everywhere. All watching. I still didn't know what was going on.

An officer approached my car and waved for me to move along. I rolled down the window and gave him my name. I told him I was called to come here.

I was taken to a police car and while in the car, driving closer to the Fire Hall, the officer explained that a group of kids were playing in the ditch and they had been caught in the culvert.

"A group of kids were playing in the ditch over there," he said, pointing in the direction of a crowd. "Two of the boys fell into the culvert. They managed to get one of them out."

He was silent, biting his lip.

"We-I'm sorry-we can't find your son. He's gone."

As we walked to the fire hall, I asked how long he had been in the culvert and was told it had been about 30 minutes.

I wasn't going to allow myself to acknowledge it. He wasn't gone. I had taken Adam to his first swimming lesson when he was 8 months old. I had watched him at his diving class. He was a strong swimmer and he was going to be fine, just a little wet.

The crowds were still watching. More police and rescue workers showed up.

I paced in and out of the Fire Hall, watching, and not believing.

I had to call Michelle. She'd know what to do. I wanted her there.

> *Other than speculation about a city works crew trying to drain water from streets in the area the night before. Rapid runoff had been blamed for flooding homes on Leila for the fifth straight year.*
>
> *All the boy's mom and dad - Rob and Kim - seemed to know for sure is what police suggested.*
> That Adam was a hero.

That's all the police knew. They had no idea that I had wanted to take Adam and Kevin for lunch but changed my mind at the last minute. They didn't have a clue that the night before Michelle (my girlfriend) and I had given him a new pair of shoes after karate class. Adam said, "Cool dad, they're just like yours."

The T-shirt that Michelle had bought him was the only thing that came out of the culvert that afternoon.

I sat for over an hour reading and reading the same articles. It seemed the more times I read them the harder it was to believe.

This was all a bad dream.

That afternoon, the afternoon that it happened was hours behind me. I remember a helpless feeling becoming overwhelming. I wanted to do something. I had to do something.

I started driving around, going nowhere. I went back to the coffee shop again and sat
for a while longer.

I bought two dozen donuts and took them to the fire hall for the fireman. Why? I had to do something.

> *Adam wasn't the only hero, though.*
>
> *Late yesterday afternoon, the four fire-fighters involved with the rescue of the boy sat together recalling what had happened.*
>
> *Capt. Cliff Sinclair, 49 and firefighters Don Shellrude, 45, Jean Paul Delorme, 33 and Terry Lamb, 46 were just finishing lunch about 12:30 when they heard the station's front doorbell ringing.*
>
> *"I went running to the door and I could hear a kid screaming," said Shellrude.*

"My friend's caught in the culvert," the frantic boy yelled.

Shellrude yelled to the others.

As he rounded the corner of the fire hall running, he could see a group of kids standing by the culvert - or ditch-yelling and screaming.

"And it was just a matter of getting there now."

"As I got closer I could see there was a kid."

It was the 11 year old Adam had been trying to rescue.

The boy was up to his chest in a whirlpool of water that was thigh-high on Shellrude.

"He was hanging on to something," Shellrude remembered. "I grabbed a hold of him."

By that time, Shellrude's buddy Delorme was in the water with him.

"Jean-Paul grabbed a hold of him and the boy proceeded to say his buddy or his friend was hanging on to his legs."

Adam was alive.

"We're hanging on to him," Shellrude said to the boy, "and we've made a bit of a sweep with our other arm as best we could. And at that point or shortly after, the kid we had a hold of said, "I can't feel him any more."

By then the lunch hour crowd had swollen to 50.

The force of the current was so strong that the boy's legs had been forced into a tuck that Shellrude and Delorme had to pry apart like a stubborn jackknife.

The boy was carried to the station house, bundled up and given a change of clothing from the firefighters' locker.

Meanwhile, the firefighters frantically searched adjacent sewer openings, hoping to find Adam.

But, as other firefighters were to learn hours later, he was gone.

What impressed the firefighters about the boy who was rescued was the way he wanted to talk only about his friend.

> *"He was just concerned about his friend,"* firefighter Terry Lamb said.
> *"That was what he was primarily upset about. It's a sad case, it really is."*

As the afternoon passed, panic started to set in. I wanted to jump in and get him myself. I didn't care that the rescue workers were tied together for safety. I wanted to go in and get him myself. I'm his Dad. It's my job.

Instead of rescuing Adam, I had to be the one to tell Marc and Kevin. How do I face them? I made the commitment the minute I set my eyes on all three of them when they were born. I was going to protect and raise them. I would always be there. Even though, their mom and I were separated, I would always be there.

Kevin, who is 12, knew that something had happened to Adam. He and Adam went to the same school. They walked to and from school together. They walked past the culvert twice a day, five days a week.

Now Kevin would be making that trip by himself. How do I tell him?

As I approached the school doors, a rush of kids ran out. All of them were crying. It was Adam's class. They had just announced to his class that he was gone. Three young girls dropped to their knees, sobbing.

Kevin was walking behind them, alone. His head was down. He hadn't been told, but
he knew. He could see it in my eyes.

I held him for the longest time, trying to take away his sobbing. But I couldn't.

We sat on the curb, not saying anything for a few minutes. We didn't have to.

"Now what, Dad?" Kevin asked.

> *Young has two younger sons, 12 and eight.*
> *"The hardest part was having to tell the two of them. That I don't have answers. That I don't know if they're going to find him."*
> *There is a final irony.*
> *Rand Shipman is another father who came*

racing to the scene when he heard what had happened.
Fortunately, his teenaged son wasn't involved.
But Shipman had a lot to say to reporters.
"This area has always been known to have an enormous amount of water in the ditches. The city doesn't seem to care. Why do we have to have an open ditch system basically running through four schools?
Shipman went on.
"I plan to contact my city councillor about doing something about this."
His councillor is Mike O'Shaughnessy.
Last night, O'Shaughnessy's wife said her husband was "just sick" about what happened.
And O'Shaughnessy was the one flooded Leila residents turned to about sending a city crew out to unplug the sewer system.
And he knew Adam.
Rob Young was O'Shaughnessy's executive assistant two years ago.
Young had been in O'Shaughnessy's office yesterday morning, just before police contacted him on his cell phone and told him there was an emergency.
He was with O'Shaughnessy's executive assistant, talking about the water.
"Oh, I wasn't complaining," Young said. "I was just talking about how bad it was with flooding that's out here and it's too bad they can't do something."

Sometime around 4:30 pm., Capt. Neil Lewis of the Salvation Army, who was acting as the go between with the rescue workers and the family, approached me, asking to have the family meet in the back room of the fire hall.

By this time friends and family had arrived and been on the scene for a few hours. How could I possibly feel so alone with all these people around?

Capt. Lewis proceeded to explain that the effort was being changed from a rescue to a recovery. Adam was gone and there wasn't much hope. I wanted to ask, "Gone where!"

The recovery effort continued for another hour and then everyone started to pack up and leave.

Why? They hadn't found him. Why were they stopping.? Where was Adam? What was I supposed to do? Where was I supposed to go?

2

Rob, what can I do? You know I'll do anything I can.
It was Mike O'Shaughnessy. Councillor Mike O'Shaughnessy.

Mike had been elected city councillor, representing the area for eighteen of the last twenty four years. I had worked for Mike for three of those years, and remained a friend
for almost eight years.

It was about 10 am and he wanted to talk.

"Mike, right now all I want is to find him and make sure this doesn't happen again," I told him.

Mike replied, "Lets grab a coffee. I want to talk to you. I just want to spent some time with you. I'll pick you up. Where are you?"

Mike showed up in about 30 minutes and we went to the local Perkins for coffee.

He couldn't even look me in the eye. He wanted to be close but remained distant.

He told me he had been in an EPC (Executive Policy Committee) meeting when someone told him there had been an accident in his ward. Some kids were playing in a ditch and one fell into an open manhole and disappeared.

Mike asked for the name.

After a few minutes they came back and told him to sit down. It was Adam Young, Rob's son.

The EPC meeting was immediately stopped and I've heard from others at City Hall, Mike ran to his office crying.

On his way to the parking lot he completely broke down and had to have someone drive him to the scene. I had been on the scene all afternoon, but I didn't see him. I'm assuming he went home when he saw the crowds on the scene.

Over coffee, Mike called the Water and Waste department and made arrangements for us to go down and speak to the director. It was kind of comforting to know that I was going to speak to the people in charge. It felt good to have friends in high places.

Everything was going to be fine. Adam would be home playing Nintendo soon.

Open Ditches Worry City

City officials are scrambling to see if they can child proof more than 100 open ditches similar to the one that swallowed a 14-year old boy on Tuesday.

Adam Young was playing in a ditch with his best friend on Leila Avenue near Manila Street when he was sucked into a culvert and into the city's sewer system. He still hasn't been found.

After meeting with city workers who are searching for his son, Adam's father learned there are more ditches in the city with open culverts.

"Let's stop it from happening again," Rob Young said yesterday. "Let's find these things and cover them up."

I don't want the people involved to waste time over who's to blame."

Not all of the ditches are an "extreme hazard" but the city will assess them and decide whether to barricade the ditches with snow fencing.

FOR MY SON

> *"We are going to deal with this as best as we can,"* said Tom Pearson, manager for the local water sewer system. *"We'll be reminding people that we're in a situation where any open water is dangerous."*
> by Melanie Verhaeghe, Winnipeg Free Press

When Mike and I arrived at the Works and Operations Head Office, I remember feeling out of place. Alienated. Not one person could look at me. They would all look down, avoiding any kind of eye contact.

We walked to the director's office, Tom Pearson.

Pearson's hand was shaking as he reached out to greet me.

"I'm so sorry for what's happened. Is there anything we can do," Pearson said.

"I need to know what happened and where he is."

Pearson explained that Adam had fallen into a land drainage inlet that connected to the storm sewer system. At the time the amount of water in the storm sewer was too much to send a crew in to look for him. They had blocked one section of the sewer line off underground and hoped to find him close by, along Manila and Jefferson.

They had placed a 45 pound sand bag at the point of entry, where Adam went in and tried to watch for it at different intervals through the manholes, but the current was so strong it completely disappeared.

He then brought out a map of the sewer system and with his finger, drew out the path they assumed Adam was going to take.

He said he could end up as far away as Kildonan Park, which was about 12 miles away. They had installed a screen at the outlet so he wouldn't end up in the river.

I asked him how long it could be until he was found.

"Because the system is at it's full capacity now, he could end up at the Armstrong Street Catch Basin anytime now. If he is caught up somewhere along the route it could be a few months before we can send someone down there to walk the system and check.

We've placed a screen across the outlet so he won't end up in the river," Pearson said, all the while trying to avoid eye contact with me. It seemed the entire conversation was directed at Mike. It's like I wasn't even there.

Mike was adamant, "I want everything done to find him."

"We have people going along the route pulling up manhole covers to see if they can find him. I assure you we're doing everything we can," Pearson said.

Mike asked, "How many of these things are out there?"

"We're not sure at this time, but we have people looking into it."

"I want these things fixed. I don't care what the cost is and I really don't care what the legal department says, they have their own agenda. Forget the reports and everything else. Just fix them. That's all we're asking."

The legal department? This should have been my first clue. I discovered, months later that the City's legal department had met the night Adam died to discuss the issue.

Pearson couldn't give us very many solid answers but the legal department had already met to discuss the issue.

It's been 18 hours since Adam disappeared. They can't tell me where he is. It's an awful feeling to drive around the city wondering if your son is floating right below you.

They can't tell me if this is going to happen again, to Kevin, Marc, Jake or Aaron (Michelle's two boys), but they can tell me the lawyers have already discussed this.

I felt sick. The only thing I could hold on to was Mike's comments. I believed things would happen.

I've got friends in high places.

3

The next few days are a blur. I can't recall exactly what I did, when, why, but I do remember an immense feeling of loneliness and helplessness.

I would get in the car and go. I had to go. I don't know where, but I had to go.

I found myself going to the site where Adam disappeared numerous times. Almost daily. I'd look at the flowers that had been placed there.

I couldn't read the cards that people left. As I would stand there, people would drive up, slow down and then drive away. Nobody would say anything.

I tried to spend as much time as I could with Marc and Kevin even though it was hard to face them. With Kim and I being separated, it was difficult. She needed Marc and Kevin around her.

Kim had her own support network around for most of the time and I didn't feel I belonged. After all, I couldn't protect my son.

> **Father Issues Tearful Warning**
>
> *Rob Young wants to make sure no other parent feels his pain.*
>
> *On Tuesday his 14-year old son, Adam*

> *was swept away by flood waters in a culvert into a manhole. Adam was the first Winnipegger to die as a result of the flood waters.*
>
> *"We have enough water, let's not have any more tears," Young said*
> *yesterday, while making a plea for everyone to stay away from all water.*
>
> *"I don't want to be able to say to another parent 'I know what you're going through.'"*
>
> *"Adam wasn't a little kid - he was 5-2, 150 pounds so it's not only children," he said.*
>
> *The public is being asked to call 911 if they see anyone near fast moving water.*
>
> *"There has been a lot of talk of blame - that isn't an issue right now. The first priority is to get him out of there," he said.*
>
> *"I have nothing but praise for the police and fire department and people at city hall."*
> *by Kevin Conner, Winnipeg Sun*

On Friday, Kevin, Marc and myself did a press conference with Mayor Thompson and Mike O'Shaughnessy. I did not want the issue of blame to become the focus. This was more of a plea.

I asked Michelle to be there for Marc and Kevin. In case things got too emotional for them, during the press conference, she could take them out away from the reporters. Really, I needed her there for me.

The feelings of loneliness, helplessness and failure were overwhelming. Most times I wanted to run. Michelle is the one that kept me going.

She didn't have to say anything. All I had to do was look at her, into her eyes. This is as close to losing a son as I hope she ever comes. She was hurting herself but her main concern was me.

She could take loneliness, helplessness and failure feelings away for a short time and I will always be grateful to her for that. She was and has been my strength during this entire ordeal, and she didn't have to do a thing. Just be herself.

When the four of us arrived at City Hall, Devi Sharma, Mike O'Shaughnessy's Executive Assistant met us in the lobby. I wanted to avoid the press who were hovering around.

We entered into the Councillor's office area and were met with the same look. People just didn't want to look us in the eyes. Several councillors offered their condolences. Bill Clement met me in the hall and shook my hand, Lillian Thomas gave me a hug.

John Angus came out and said, "I can't even look at you or I'll start crying. I'm sorry."

At the end of the press conference, Mayor Thompson asked the media and the public to respect our families privacy and give us time to grieve. The room went deadly silent.

Again people in the room just could not look at us directly.

The talk of a law suit had already started. One of Kim's cousins had contacted a lawyer he said on our behalf. That's the last thing I wanted to even think about. I didn't want people to start talking defensive action to protect themselves. I wanted him found and I wanted the City to take remedial measures to the similar sites in the city.

Things weren't happening fast enough. Publicly I was quiet and calm. Inside I was falling apart.

I kept having nightmares of Adam holding onto the sides of the culvert screaming, "Dad, please help me." It got to the point where I was scared to sleep. I didn't. I avoided sleep as much as I could.

I headed to a shopping centre just to get away.

It felt like everyone was staring at me. Several people approached me to offer their condolences. All strangers.

One man pulled me aside and said, "I can't imagine what you're going through but I have to thank you. I have 3 kids and because of what's happened and what you've said they won't even go near a puddle. Thank you."

I wanted to run.

I appreciated what he said, but it didn't help. My son was dead. I may have helped this father but I failed my son.

How could you feel so lonely in a crowded shopping centre?

I don't remember what it was that I bought at the mall, but I do remember the clerk saying, "Oh my God, it's you! You're not paying for this, you've given enough."

4

"There will be a memorial service for Adam Young at 1:00 this afternoon at the McGregor Armoury, on the corner of Machray Ave. and McGregor in our city under siege.

A gentle 14-year old boy who's dream was to be a pilot. His young body, dragged down by the flood waters has yet to be found.

In a time of hardship and need, when so many unknown people are openly giving of their time, effort and money to help so many other unknown people, in a time of disaster for so many evacuees, the whole community of Winnipeg has been taught a lesson in life by the quiet, honest public comments made by Adam's father, Rob.

They will never bring Adam back to dad Rob, mother Kim, his brother's Kevin or Marc, or many other relatives, friends or schoolmates. But the incredible strength of the entire Young family on this April 28, 1997 epitomizes human-

ity under the worst of all nightmares, the death of a child.

The flood forces of Mother Nature have taken a young boy from us, but they have not been able to break Rob Young's human spirit, and at 1:00 this afternoon, a city will remember Adam.
-One Man's Opinion, Peter Warren, CJOB

Strength? Human spirit? What does he mean? I couldn't save my son. Adam's gone and they're calling me strong.

The nightmares are becoming more prevalent. They're happening during the day when I'm wide awake.

I still visit the site everyday trying to say goodbye, but really I'm hoping he'll come crawling out of the culvert or maybe some manhole somewhere. I'll take him home and as only Adam would, drop his wet clothes by the door and start watching TV from his chair, questioning what all the fuss was all about.

On Saturday, I was told the church was going to hold a memorial service for Adam. Friends and relatives had come in from out of town, and according to some, needed to get on with things.

This would be their time to say goodbye. It wasn't mine.

The memorial service was held at McGregor Armoury. This was where Adam went to Cadets every Friday night and Saturday afternoon. More importantly, this was the place where one of Adam's dreams was being fulfilled. To be a pilot.

And that was just one of his dreams, one small part of his life. The faces of over 800 people in attendance reflected a lot more.

Walking into the armoury, I avoided the eyes of the people standing, and I tried not to listen to what people were saying about my son.

Hundreds say goodbye to drowned teen
Adam Young used to go to the McGregor Armoury several times a week, where he was an air cadet and part of the drill team, flag party and a member of the band.

The 14-year old wanted to be a pilot, and he hoped to put himself through university by working as a life guard.

FOR MY SON

> *Yesterday afternoon, more than 700 people turned out at the Armoury to say goodbye to Adam. One week ago today, he was sucked into a culvert and into the city's sewer system.*
> *"I hope you're not here looking for answers. I have none, and we'll find none this side of eternity," Rev. Bob Shelton of Garden Park Baptist Church told a memorial service.*
> Glen MacKenzie, Winnipeg Free Press

I could see parts of Adam's life in everyone that was there.

Jeff, Don and Doug from karate, Don Bell, who's daughter, Kim was one of Adam's first babysitters, Adam's classmates most of whom I'd never met but knew their names, Tania, the girl he'd had a mad crush on, and hundreds more.

All these people represent a part of Adam's life. A small part. The bigger parts were supposed to come. At 14, he was just beginning. Dreams were just dreams so far, forming into reality.

For me, reality still hadn't sunk in.

After the service, friends and relatives gathered around to offer their condolences. It was a swarm of people, all trying to take the pain away. All trying to say the right thing.

People I haven't seen since high school were approaching me. City Councillors, MLA's, MP's are shaking my hand, giving out hugs like they really cared.

I can see Michelle standing off by herself. The crowd is moving me farther and farther away. I can't see her eyes, I feel lost, alone and scared.

What do I do? What do you say to these people?

Thanks for coming? I'm not grateful for anyone coming. I'm not even grateful I'm here. I wanted to run. As far away from here as possible.

5

The next day, after the memorial service, I visited the site where Adam died. This was becoming a daily ritual for me, but today was different.

I found a note among all the others. I'd never read the other notes and cards that had been left at the site before as I felt they were private messages from the person who left them and Adam. For some reason I picked this one.

> *"Dear Adam.*
> *I did not know you but I feel bad.*
> *You are a hero, and I bless you.*
> *Megan."*

I found the note, in the snow, next to a bouquet of flowers.

One of Adam's dream's was to be a life guard. To help others. I now knew he had succeeded.

He had shown us just how dangerous these culverts, drainage inlets really were. And in his own way, he was going to stop this from happening again.

He was a lifeguard. A real hero and I wasn't going to let him or his deed be forgotten.

A few days later, the Winnipeg Sun published the note from Megan as a lead in to one of their stories. They titled it, "An epitaph for Adam. - Note tribute to flood hero."

About a week later, I received a letter from Megan's mother that had been passed on to me through a church.

It read,

> Dear Mr. Young
> This is Megan
> (a school photo was attached)....
>
> The little girl who did not know your son. She's a very sensitive child and her note to your son, was written form her heart.
>
> From the very beginning of this terrible tragedy, I've had a hurt tugging at my heart. I can't, and no one can possibly imagine what you have gone through. It's a very high price you've had to pay to have your son be a hero.
>
> I've gone by and stood at the water many times over the past week and I can only ask 'Why? One of my sons' goes to Leila North as well, but he did not know Adam either. But when I heard there had been an accident, my heart stopped. I soon found out who was missing, but my heart kept tugging.
>
> I know that many people attended the memorial service on April 28. I didn't attend, but I did go to the water later that day to say goodbye.
>
> But when I neared the spot, I saw two people getting out of a car with a very large and beautiful flower arrangement, and I watched for a brief moment as the two people stood there. I could only presume that it was you and Adam's mother. I left, as I thought it was not my place to be there at that moment. I felt terrible inside.
>
> Then last week we went for a drive to the Forks and Megan noticed some tulips just lying on the grass. There was 5 of the flowers, and if left there, they would only wilt away. She wanted to have one so she could leave it for Adam. In the car she asked me for a piece of paper, so I ripped off the end of an envelope

FOR MY SON

and she proceeded to write her note.

She was quiet all the way back and as she got out of the car I helped her put the flowers and the note on the orange fencing.

I knew it meant a lot to her to have been able to do that. I was very proud of her. She too knew how much the accident bothered me.

On Friday I had a day off work, and once again, I went for a walk to the water. I went and stood there for a few minutes. I only prayed that they would find Adam soon. With so many people watching the rising river, I wondered why he had not been found.

Later that day I heard that someone had been found. The next day I knew who! I was relieved to some extent, but that tugging at my heart persisted.

At work on Tuesday morning, one of my co-workers turned to me and asked me how my daughter spelled her name. Then she proceeded to tell me about the article in the Winnipeg Sun on Sunday. I went and picked up a paper and read the note. I went home and showed my daughter.

She was so happy to know that her little note meant something to you. She read the article over and over again. To me it was a small sign from someone above. Of all the notes and cards you read and could have picked up, you chose hers.

I don't know or even want to know the pain of such a loss. I have felt pain, but I know it comes no where near yours.

But my pain was relieved a bit because in some very small way, my daughter, a little 10 year old, touched your heart with a few words from our hearts.

Take care Mr. Young, of yourself and your other 2 boys, and believe as I do, that Adam will always be watching over you and them.

He is and always will be a hero to everyone.
Thank you Adam.
Megan's Mother, Katherine.
I have never met Megan or her mother.
I have not heard from them since the letter I received.
But I do know they're out there.

6

"Hi, Rob. It's Ian Mann from District 6 Police Department. They've asked me to call you because I know you. I'm letting you know before you hear it on the radio, that we've found a body in the Armstrong Street Catch Basin and we think it might be Adam."

It was about 4:30 pm. on Friday May 2 when I received another phone call form the police.

I went home and listened to the radio and waited for another phone call. I tried not to think of the next step. Identifying the body of my son.

The call came about an hour later. The officer explained that they had found a body in the catch basin. They were taking it to the Health Science Center and someone from the Medical Examiner's office would call if they thought it was Adam.

I couldn't do it. I was still having the nightmares. Still seeing his face screaming, "Dad please help me."

I had told Michelle about the nightmares that I had been having a few days prior. She said she didn't see it that way. She saw Adam's chubby little face, with his mischievous smile looking down at us. Looking down and watching over all of us, and that's what I had been focusing on and it was helping.

Susan Hamilton, a member of the Medical Examiner's office called a short time later. She started to ask questions about Adam.

What kind of watch was he wearing? It was one that Michelle and I had given him for Christmas. Did he have a key chain. Yes, It was a another gift from us. And the necklace was a gift from his mom.

Susan asked me to come down and identify him. I knew I couldn't do it.

I had thought about having to do this for a while. Now that the time had come I realized that I wasn't able to do it. I couldn't bring myself to identify my own son's body.

I was having those nightmares and trying to focus on what Michelle had said and I didn't want anything to change Michelle's vision.

I called Ward and Caroline (Adam's aunt and uncle) and Tim Potter and Helen Clark, (two very close friends). They agreed to do this for me.

I had decided to not tell Adam's mom, Kim, until we knew for sure it was him. Then we would let her make her own decision.

We met in the waiting room of the Health Science Centre. Michelle, Ward, Caroline, Tim, Helen and myself. Susan and two police officers took down everyone's names and particulars. Then the walk started.

We took the elevator down to the basement of the Health Science Center.

The walk was haunting. The hallway seemed to go on forever. It was cold and our footsteps echoed on. I can still hear that sound today. When I do think of it and hear the steps, it still brings me to tears.

Ward, Caroline, Tim and Helen went into a room together. I stayed out and waited.

When they started to file out, they didn't have to say anything. Each one came out, one by one. As they came out, their head's were down. They'd look up at me, then look at the floor again.

Ward was the first to speak. "He looks like he's sleeping," he said. Helen tried to look at me but all she said "He's looks very peaceful."

I turned and walked away, saying nothing It was Adam. It sunk in now.

7

Drowning spurs culvert check

Adam Young's death by drowning sparked a city-wide inspection of hundreds of open culverts.

An inquest may be called into the teen's death, the province's chief medical examiner said yesterday.

"It will be considered, but first I want to get all the reports," Dr. Peter Markesteyn said.

"Some culverts must be left unscreened," Mayor Susan Thompson said. "They're a certain size and if a screen is put on, it will catch debris and defeat the purpose," Thompson said.

Inspectors were out yesterday to see if culverts could be made safer.

Witnesses questioned why the culvert was

> left exposed and why there were no warning signs.
> "This just draws kids in, and the city doesn't seem to care," parent Rand Shipman said.
> No one is to blame, local water and sewer manager, Tom Pearson said.
> "The system worked the way it was supposed to, and in a normal year it would be fairly benign," Pearson said.
> "People just assume what was safe in the past is safe this year. But I understand why people would be concerned, and what we have to do is learn from experience."

We were going to work together. The city and myself were going to work to make sure this never happens again. I started to get to it.

I had so many questions going through my mind, I didn't know where to start.

Why did this happen? How could Adam, who was about 5'2" and weighed almost 150 pounds been swept into a culvert? Why was this culvert in an area around a school?

Where were the teachers or supervisors? It was lunch time, there should have been supervision.

My first step was to contact Tom Pearson, Manager for the Water and Waste Department.

I went to his office and asked for the specifications of land drainage systems. They must have some guidelines for when developer's develop property and have to connect these new areas to existing systems and services. Who pays for it?

Pearson explained that they did have specifications and guidelines and he would forward them to me as soon as he could.

Something had happened. Pearson didn't seem like the same person. He was evasive. Cold. Annoyed that I had even showed up.

I left feeling awkward. Something wasn't right.

I called a friend of mine who is an engineer at a major development company in Winnipeg. He told me the city has guidelines and specifications that they update and send out to the developers on a yearly basis.

He also said that if his company had developed that particular site, it would never have been like that.

Now it started.

He gave me several names of professionals who could possibly help with some investigation and any questions I may have had.

I called a fellow named Ken Moore at UMA Engineering. He seemed reluctant to talk, but assured me that UMA was not an expert in the field of Land Drainage or civil engineering and referred me back to City Hall.

"They're the ones who know what's going on," he said. "We're not experts in this field."

8

It's not something that any parent thinks about. It never crosses your mind. There isn't a school, a book or training video out there that can help with this. A parent shouldn't have to make this type of decision. It's not the way it's supposed to be.

The Medical Examiner's office wanted to know what to do with my son's body. Adam's life was now contained in a clear plastic bag on the desk. The possessions that he had with him. His watch, the key chain and the necklace. That's it. 14 years all in a bag.

Jim Hull, the director of the Medical Examiner's office invited me in. He told me Adam's death had shaken everyone in the office.

He had heard about the accident on the radio on his way home from work, and immediately thought of his own kids. He was outraged that this was allowed to happen. Jim would turn out to be a very valuable ally.

Jim explained the process that his office was going to go through. He also told me that Susan Hamilton, one of the best investigators in the province, had been assigned to handle Adam's file.

The autopsy was done on that weekend and they were waiting for the final reports to be done.

I told Jim that one of the media outlets had mentioned an inquest may be called.

He explained that once every six or eight weeks a committee meets and discusses all the accidental deaths during that time. The committee then makes a decision on whether an inquest is necessary. This meeting would not be until the beginning of June to give all the parties time to submit their reports.

Mean while a funeral had to be planned.

It's not something I wanted to do. I didn't know where to start or who to talk to.

Kim also had a difficult time . It took us several tries to plan the funeral.

Tim Potter, a close friend agreed to do most of the planning. All we had to do was make some final decisions. He laid out the options for us and somehow the plans were done.

Klassen's Funeral Home were donating it's services. Everyone made this step as easy as possible.

Marc and Kevin made the decision to say their final goodbye to Adam on their own. But they wanted me there.

They had gathered some of Adam's favorite things so he could take them with him. They chose his favorite teddy bear and some other items that Adam had gathered. I bought him his favorite donut, for the last time.

I had been teaching Adam how to play the guitar. I gave him an electric one for his birthday just a few weeks prior. Everytime we got together to play, he never had his own guitar pick. I had brought him one and Marc placed it in Adam's hand.

I couldn't get close to the coffin. It was too much. I stayed back with Kevin, who also couldn't get close.

"He was a good guy, eh Dad," Kevin said, as a tear rolled down his cheek.

9

On June 11, Jim Hull called to say the medical examiner's report was done. I had told him earlier that I wanted a copy of the report and he said I was allowed to have one.

During our conversation, he said he had received all the reports he needed, the last one was a report from the city and that had just arrived. I asked for a copy of it, but was denied because of a disclaimer that the city's legal department had put at the end of the report.

Jim left the office to get a coffee and the city's report was right there. I grabbed it and started to read.

Three pages. That's it. Two pages of print and a drawing. After almost two months of investigating, all the city could come up with was three pages. I was shocked.

It contained comments like,

"this type of installation does not, in our experience, present a hazard to the public."

In this report, it said that the culvert where Adam had died was secured.

"Immediately after the accident, the culvert at Leila where Young was drawn in was covered with chain-link fencing and barricaded."

Snow fence and chicken wire had been placed around the site. That's it. I knew because I had been there almost daily.

The drawing that the city engineers had submitted was crude and inaccurate. The water level indicated was only about four inches deep.

The document also indicated that new policies would be in place shortly. To be precise,

"within the next one month period."

The report also went on to say,

"A Directive was subsequently issued to field staff who maintain the land drainage system to locate and make secure any similar installations"

When Jim came back to the office, I didn't know what to say. I wasn't supposed to have seen this. I wasn't allowed to know the information that was contained in this report. What do I do? The report was a lie!

Fuck it! This was my son and they were lying about. Something was being covered up. Why weren't they telling the truth.

I told Jim that I looked at the report.

First of all the site where Adam had died was not secured. Someone had put an orange plastic snow fence around the site and then stuck a piece of chicken wire in the opening on the evening he had died. It was now taken down.

The drawing that had been submitted showing four inches of water was wrong. There was at least 3 feet of water in the ditch when he died.

I needed to prove it.

I wasn't allowed to see the file that had been compiled by the medical examiner's office. Other than the city's report, I didn't know what was in there and what was being said.

My first step was to prove to Hull's office that the drawing that had been submitted was far from accurate. The water level was higher and the angles and dimensions of the site were wrong.

The media had been covering the story of Adam's death on almost a daily basis. I would get at least 2 calls a day from one of them, asking for updates on the whole situation. They should have something I could use.

I contacted the Winnipeg Fee Press Photo Editor, Jon Thorvaldson.. I explained to him what I wanted. He told me he had been at the site on the afternoon that Adam died and had taken several rolls of film and suggested I come down and look through them.

The pictures were great. They showed the water level from several different angles. Some showed the rescue effort and you could see the difficulty the rescue team was having. In some pictures the water level was at their waist, they were tethered together with safety lines and the manholes had sandbagged dikes around them to keep the water out.

"Take whatever you need," Jon said.

Next I contacted Andrew Smith. Andrew is a police officer assigned to the Victim Services Department. He deals with victims of crimes and accidents and he seems to act more as a social worker than an officer.

He knew a bit about my background as a counsellor and on the day of the accident, made an assumption that was wrong.

The Winnipeg Police had sent out several social workers, counsellors and Andrew to the scene of the accident while the rescue attempt was going on. After Capt. Lewis broke the news to us that the rescue was being changed to a recovery, Andrew approached me, not knowing why I was there and said, "Boy, did you get here fast."

He assumed that I was there in a professional capacity.

"It was my son that went down there," I said, with my head down.

An awkward moment of silence followed.

"I lost my daughter a few months ago. I'm sorry," he said.

"Let me know if there's anything I can do. You know my number".

I called Andrew, requesting to see the police report.

I met him downtown, at the Public Safety Building. He entered the room without the police report. He told me I couldn't see the report without permission. He told me he had just finished reading it and he would answer any questions that I had. I wanted to know what had happened. I still didn't have any details.

He told me that a group of kids, including Adam had been playing in the ditch. Adam and another boy Justin Jones were chasing a piece of styrofoam in the water and Adam fell in.

This wasn't good enough. I wanted that report. This wasn't

getting me anywhere.

I was starting to feel left out. No police report. No access to the medical examiner's file and what I did see in the file was wrong.

I took the Free Press photos and pictures of the site as it was that day to Hull. Because of his position, Jim couldn't say too much. But I knew what he was thinking. There was going to be an inquest.

The city was not going to take responsibility for what happened.

People assume that the elected officials are ones who make the decisions. Not true.

I had sympathy and assurances from almost every political figure at City Hall. But this was talk. Nothing concrete was happening. Things were stalled.

I thought I had friends downtown. After all, I had worked for several city counsellors, done projects for the mayor. I knew them personally and professionally. Adam had baby-sat for the O'Shaughnessys'. John Angus had given us is cottage for a week one summer. Adam called him Grampa Angus. John had taken him and Marc and Kevin for a boat ride one day. I wasn't just a citizen, I was a friend.

The day of the accident, I was in O'Shaughnessy's office talking to him about a position. The position was the Safe City Coordinator.

He had suggested I consider this position and told me I would have Council's support if I was interested.

In mid June, I started to consider it. I needed to get on with my life. There wasn't anything else I could do with respect to Adam's death. I thought of him and the accident daily. But I needed to get on with things.

I started back at City Hall doing special projects, and acting as an Executive Assistant. I was also working to get things going with the Safe City position. I learned that there were things that had to be done prior to the position starting. I did have the support from most of Council. Everyone of the politicians I spoke to about it agreed that I was the ideal candidate. I knew and worked with all of them in the past. I had been one of the few people who could work at both the political and administrative levels simultaneously and still get the job done.

While going through the discussions about the safe city committee, several councillors offered me small contract projects. This kept me busy for a month or two.

More importantly, it allowed me to be back in the group, in the circle.

One morning when I arrived, I looked at my desk and saw a file laying right on top. Someone had placed it there. It contained some interesting information.

There was several documents pertaining to the site where Adam had died.

There was a copy of a letter to Mike O'Shaughnessy from someone who lives on Leila, across from where Adam had died. It was written by Wayne Benedit. Benedit had submitted, although fairly rough, a set of drawings of a cover for open drainage inlets. He went on to discuss the advantages and the disadvantages of his design and requested that the city look at his design. Attached to his letter was a letter to Tom Pearson from O'Shaughnessy, asking him to look into Benedit's submission and to report back to him. The letter from Benedit was dated on April 22, two days after the accident. Pearson never did report back.

Along with Benedit's letter and drawings, the file contained phone record log and a stack of phone messages from another resident, Paul Wereschuk. From the dates on the messages, Wereschuk had called O'Shaughnessy's office several times in the days prior to the accident and several times afterward.

I was dumb founded, Shocked. I got on the phone to Wereschuk.

I met with him the next day. He told me he had been complaining about the area for several years. Water levels and flooding had been a problem off and on since 1993, and nothing had been done.

In the days prior to Adam's death, he had tried to get a hold of O'Shaughnessy several times. On one called him back or responded to his requests.

He then tried Harry Lazarenko. Lazarenko is the councillor who's ward is next to Mike's. Harry has been the longest standing member of city council and is well known.

It turned out that Harry was at the site 2 days before Adam died. Harry made the appropriate calls to the Water and Waste Department. He had requested assistance from the Emergency Department and assumed the department had responded.

Wereschuk, frustrated from the lack of response, called the

Mayor's office on Monday April 19. He told Susan Thompson's secretary about the situation.

"If something isn't done, someone is going to get hurt," Wereschuk said.

Benedit informed me that other than a letter confirming his fax and saying that his drawing was forwarded to the Water and Waste department, he had not received any other feedback from the city.

They knew.

City Hall was aware of the site, but they did nothing. Adam didn't have to die. It could have been prevented.

10

Inquest Planned Into Teen's Death
There will be an inquest into the death of Winnipeg teen Adam Young, Manitoba's chief medical examiner has announced.

Young, 14, died on April 22 when he was sucked into an open culvert.

His body was recovered on May 2 at the Armstrong and Main Diversion Plant.

"I'm glad they've finally decided to go ahead," said Rob Young, who has been pushing for the inquest to try to prevent more accidents like the one that claimed his son."

"I made a commitment to my other two children that this would never happen to anyone else.

I'm not going to let go of that."
Tod Mohamed, Winnipeg Sun, June 25, 1997

The inquest was announced. This would be our chance to make some points. The issue of safety, the lack of standards, a public forum to show people just how the system that they had created responds to issues.

What most people didn't know was how hard I pushed for the inquest.

I proved to the medical examiner's office investigators that the information that the city had given them was false. The drawings were inaccurate, they hadn't done anything to prevent this from happening again.

The city hadn't even sent anyone out to inspect the site. They had no idea even how big the opening of the pipe was. In the report that was sent, they estimated the size.

I had spoken to a civil engineering professor at the University of Manitoba. He was familiar with the site as he had gone to inspect it for his own information. He claimed, based on a computer model he had developed, the force at the opening of the drainage outlet was around 200 pounds of pressure.

After 2 months, the city had not made an effort to any remedial measures. Kevin and I fixed several culverts that were similar in construction. We fixed the one where Adam had died.

I had applied for standing at the inquest, which means myself or a lawyer had input into creating the witness list. We could also question the witnesses that were to be called.

The Crown had appointed Kelly Moar to act on their behalf. Kelly would run the inquest.

At the beginning of August, I applied to the city for some of the reports concerning the accident. I applied through the Access to information Act. The act stipulates that the city administration had to reply within 30 days of my request. The 30 days would bring it into the beginning of September, allowing us time to go over all the information before the inquest.

I requested all reports from the Water and Waste Department, the police report, and any other reports pertaining to Adam's death.

"I'll process these right now Rob," Dorothy Broughton, the head of City Clerks.

The next day she told me the requests had been processed and I would be hearing something soon.

On the 30th day, a letter was delivered. It arrived by courier at 7:00 that evening.

It was not the response I expected. They were denying my

request for information.

> "Please be advised that we must deny your request for these records as stipulated in Subsections 7(l) (f) and (g) of the Access to Information By-Law (6420/94). This Subsection states that the City Administrator shall deny access if the record contains information, the disclosure of which may be prejudicial to existing or anticipated legal proceedings in which the City may be a party or information, the disclosure of which may violate solicitor/client privilege."

This letter was signed by Barry MacBride, the director of Water and Waste, and carbon copied to Marvin Samphir, Senior Counsel for the City of Winnipeg.

They claimed the information contained in these reports could lead to a potential lawsuit. I'd said for months, I was not suing. All I wanted was answers.

I was furious, hurt. I couldn't shake that feeling of failure. Being alone trying to fight something that had been done. Now what?

The next morning, Gerald Fast, the host of a local radio talk show called. Perfect timing.

Gerald wanted to know what was going on with the situation. Were they being fixed. What was the city and the school division doing?

What could I say?

"Nothing. I have no idea what their doing. Last night I received a letter from the city denying me access to any information. They claim it could lead to a law suit," I said.

"Rob, can you come on the air first thing this morning," Gerald asked.

"There's nothing to say. Nothings happening. I don't think there's a story."

"That's the story. Nothing's happening," he said.

At 9 that same morning we were on the air. I remember Gerald opening the show with a comment about this show being an emotional topic. He started off filling in the listeners about the story and who I was. He talked about how much this story affected him. He has two kids and couldn't comprehend what I was going through.

Then the callers started. They stared to slam Susan Thompson, City Hall and anyone associated with them. I remember a caller named Morris asking if I had felt deceived by my so called friends at City Hall. I was a member of "The Inner Circle", but not anymore

Another caller, she sounded older, probably a grandmother, crying so hard I couldn't understand what she was saying.

I didn't bend. I was going to be the nice guy. I came to City Hall's rescue with several callers.

These were my friends they were talking about. The people who were helping me get this job done. The politicians didn't write that letter. They probably didn't even know the letter had been sent.

I got home later that morning. Michelle had listened to the radio show and I wanted her opinion.

"You're too nice," she said. "It was obvious you were defending them."

"I know but I have to. It's the only way anything is going to happen. If I start, then the doors are going to close and everything's going to shut down. Just wait and see what's going to happen," I said.

That same morning a letter from the police department arrived. Same thing.

It said;

> *"Pursuant to the Access to Information By-Law subsection 7 (1)(f), the Winnipeg Police Service is not prepared to release the requested documents. This subsection states that the City Administrator shall deny access if the record contains: information the disclosure of which may be prejudicial to existing or anticipated legal proceedings in which the City may be a party."*

"I couldn't have a copy of the police report because of a potential lawsuit.

It did go on to say,

> *"However, given your particular circumstances, the Winnipeg Police Service is prepared, if you are agreeable, to have you attend my office at an arranged time, where you will*

be permitted to read the police reports."

This letter was signed by Gordon Schumacher, Legal Counsel for the Winnipeg Police Service. It was not carbon copied to the City's legal department.

I called immediately and set up the appointment a few days later.

The next day, I went into City Hall to work on one of the projects I had been given. I ran into Harry Lazarenko.

"Rob do what you have to do, sue if you want, just don't let them do to you what they did to the Blands'. They destroyed that family. I don't even think they live in the city anymore," Lazarenko said.

On July 11, 1984 Ian Bland, a nine year old boy, along with his mother and sister were waiting for a bus on Portage Ave., when an underground transformer exploded. Fire and hot oil roared through a grate in the sidewalk engulfing the three.

Ian suffered burns to 95 per cent of his body and died three months later in hospital.

His mother, Jocelyn Bland and his sister, Angela, 12 suffered burns and took months to recover. Some people say Jocelyn has still not fully recovered.

The Bland family settled after six years of legal wrangling with the city. They were denied access to information, stalled because of so called engineers reports and anything else the city legal department could think of.

"Harry, I don't want to sue. I just want those things fixed, but all they think about is this so called potential lawsuit."

He looked at me and said, "Now your going to find out who really runs this city. I tried to bring up the issue at the last Works and Operations meeting and Clement said if we fix them it's going to look like we're liable. Shit, we can't even talk about. They're so scared about a lawsuit that, that's all they think about"

I was nervous about having done the call in radio program the day before. I didn't know what the reaction was going to be. I found out fast.

One of the City Councillors walked in. He had heard me on Gerald Fast's show.

"You prick. Finish what you're doing and get out."

I tried to be the nice guy. I tried to work with them. I said I wasn't going to sue. Look where it got me. So much for high placed friends.

I went home and cried.

11

The appointment was set. Two days after the confrontation at City Hall, I went to the Public Safety Building to see the police report. When I got to there, Gordon Schumaker, the police department's legal counsel took me and the report to a small private room.

He placed the report on the table in front of me. This was it. This stack of papers had the answers I was looking for. It was all here. 62 pages of answers.

The first thing I noticed as I started to read was black felt pen. Big black lines through almost everything. Every place where a name was supposed to be, was now blacked out. I tried to "read between the lines".

In most of the cases, I knew who the report was referring to. I knew their titles which were not covered, but their comments in the report were there.

Comments like, "New policies would be in place within two weeks," and "similar sites would be repaired by mid June," were made by some city officials. This was now the end of August and they hadn't even fixed the one where Adam died. Kevin and I did that in June.

Another section indicated that two city workers were in the

area at the time of the accident. They had unplugged the culvert moments before Adam and his friends started playing in the ditch. They had done this everyday for the past few days. How could they have unplugged it and then just left it? Why didn't they tell the kids not to play in the water?

There was a statement from a manager, unfortunately his name was blanked out. He claimed Adam's body was swept away through the sewer within minutes. Yet they spent hours searching one particular area.

There was the statements from Adam's friends, detailing what had happened. I couldn't read them. That was too much. Too close and too painful.

The rest made me mad.

After 3 hours of reading, I went home, Upset and confused. Again, there were no answers, just more questions.

That same day, a package arrived at home in the mail from the Manitoba Department of Justice. In was a letter saying that because I had applied for standing at the inquest, I was entitled to copies of the justice department's file. Everything they had, I now had.

The letter went on to say the package contained the autopsy report, the Water and Waste report and the police report.

The Water and Waste report was the same one I had seen in Jim Hull's office. Now I had it. I could prove to other people exactly what I had been saying for months.

I looked at the police report. Something was wrong. It wasn't the same report that I had just seen a few hours ago. I checked again. It was smaller. Statements were missing.

I remember looking at the first police report. It had the pages hand numbered at the bottom of each page. 62 pages. The number stuck in my head.

I counted the pages of the report that the justice department sent me. There was 28.

Everything that had to do with a City of Winnipeg employee, manager or spokesman was gone. Someone had left out 34 pages.

I called the justice department to ask them if a mistake had been made. The secretary checked their files and called back to confirm that their file contained a 28 page police report.

Somehow between the police department and the justice department, 34 pages went missing I checked again. It wasn't the first 34, or the last 34, or even the middle 34. It was 34 random pages. They had been pulled out.

I called the someone at City Hall. I explained the mistake. Again I was being nice, giving them a chance.

"It's your word against ours'," she said, just before hanging up.

12

Culvert delay Riles Father

Almost two months after Adam Young was sucked into a culvert and drowned, the city has not identified every open ditch or come up with a permanent solution to the problem.

"It' been almost two months since the accident. Nobody seems to want to provide any answers," said Adam's father, Rob Young. All I asked for when they found him was to make sure it doesn't happen again."

"We've been asking people to identify those sites and we've only had one come in," said city sewer and water engineer, Dan Wiwchar. "We don't have people out looking for the sites. We have other programs we're behind on. We've just come out of fighting the flood."

Young can't believe finding the culverts is not a priority. "I was under the impression that was happening," Young said. "I guess children's lives aren't a priority."

Not only was I under the impression it was being done, but I was told it was. O'Shaughnessy told them to do it.

The city told the Justice Department it was being done. That's what the Water and Waste report that Jim Hull received stated.

What happened to this "directive" that was sent out?

> People living near where Adam disappeared said the city has been told for the past two years about the culvert and now it has a responsibility to ensure every culvert is safe.
>
> "I don't care if there are 10,000 of them. We're talking about children's lives," said Wayne Benedet. Benedet also sent the city ideas about how to cover the culverts, but nothing has been done.
>
> "If they're just sitting back and saying: 'Yeah, this is a problem but we're waiting for people to scream about it,' well, that's just not good enough.
>
> Paul Wereschuk's basement flooded by sewer back up across the street from the culvert. He also warned the city the day before Adam's death that someone would get hurt.
>
> A lawsuit against the city is still in the works, Young said.
>
> Coun. Harry Lazarenko said he will raise the issue of open culverts at the next works and operations meeting in three weeks.
>
> "I'm not looking at grandstanding but everytime I look at a culvert, I see that boy," he said.
>
> Meanwhile, the province's inquest review committee meets on Friday to decide which deaths warrant a closer look by calling an inquest. Adam's death is one of them.
>
> "I will strongly suggest that an inquest should be called. There are certain questions

FOR MY SON

left unanswered," said Jim Hull, director of the Chief Medical Examiner's office. "We're not trying to find fault with individuals or institutions. What we're trying to do is ensure it doesn't happen again."

By Melanie Verhaeghe, Winnipeg Free Press

City negligent says dead son's father.

The city could face criminal negligence charges and a lawsuit from the frustrated father of a 14-year old boy who drowned after being sucked into a culvert in April.

Rob Young say's he's talking legal action after five months of waiting for the city to prevent access to it's drainage systems. He also plans to sue the Seven Oaks School Division.

"I'm not getting anywhere being nice," Young said yesterday, adding the city hasn't returned his phone calls and has denied his requests for information.

He's even taken it upon himself to fix the open culvert that swallowed his son Adam on April 22.

Adam was playing in a ditch with his friend near Ecole Leila North, when he was swept into the sewer system by strong flood waters.

Concerned the hole still posed a danger to children, especially with school starting, Young secured a bar across the hole last month.

Two more bars have been placed over the hole by other concerned citizens.

He's at a loss to explain why the city hasn't taken steps to secure culverts.

We have spent more time and money saving property because of the flood," said Young. "Why can't we spent $3.50 to fix something like this?"

The city is waiting for the results of the inquest next month and an independent engineering study before making changes to it's culverts, said Bill Carroll, commissioner of works and operations.

They're safe as can be right now," Carroll said yesterday, adding there is no great water flow, there is no danger.
He said residents should not be making their own home-made repairs.

"It requires an engineered solution," Carroll said.

The city and Seven Oaks School Division have been notified of the lawsuit said Young's lawyer, Dave Guttman.

There are cases of negligence against both parties - the city for not making the culverts safe and the school for not providing noon hour supervision, Guttman said.

However the suit won't be formally filed until after the inquest into Adam's death, scheduled for Oct. 14-15, Guttman said.

School board chairman Ben Zaidman wouldn't comment on the suit, saying only it is being handled by the division's insurance company.

A letter requesting criminal negligence charges be laid against the city, with supporting information was sent Friday to Rob Finlayson,
provincial head of prosecutions.

"Mr. Young's concerns have to be addressed," said Finlayson, adding a decision on charges will be made once the letter and its information is reviewed.
By Kevin Conner, Winnipeg Sun

I started taking action. I was tired of being the nice guy. I was sick of being lied to. I felt like people were patting me on the head and saying everything will be fine, now just go away.

Well, I'm not going away. Adam didn't have to die. If people had of done their job properly he would still be here.

I contacted Dave Guttman. Dave was a lawyer who I had met about 10 years ago. I had never used Dave professionally before. Our relationship had been that of friendship for the past decade.

I called Dave not because of his reputation as a lawyer, his experience or his knowledge, but because he was a friend. I needed to work with someone I could trust, someone I could talk to but more important at this point, was someone who would let me do what I had to do.

I had trusted enough people and felt like I had been burned by them. I trusted the system to fix the situation and it let me down. I trusted the system to care for my children and it failed. This was the same system I helped create and promote.

I knew that if I started to speak out publicly, my career at City Hall would be over. I could never go back. Regardless of what some of the politicians were saying, there was no way I would be considered for any position at or associated with the city.

It's a decision I made and would have to live with. What I couldn't live with was the thought of Adam' death not having a purpose. He couldn't live with the thought of another child succumbing to the same fate as Adam. I couldn't face a father going through the same thing I was experiencing.

Bill Carroll, the commissioner of works and operations said it is going to take an "engineered solution". If an engineered solution is needed, why did the city wait until August to contact an engineer.

Why did Kevin and I fix the culvert where Adam died with 2 simple bars across the opening? It seemed to work fine.

Wayne Benedet sent drawings of an example to the city in April. He still hadn't had a response from the city.

One day while driving in an area of the city, Charleswood, I came across a culvert running under a major street, Roblin Blvd. This culvert was covered with a grid cover. This cover had been there for a while. I could tell it wasn't a new installation by the rust and wear that showed.

Why was nothing being done?

I wasn't sitting back any longer. I was going to take action.

I spoke to Rob Finlayson, the head of prosecutions for the province.

"If this had happened on private property, after several warnings, someone would be charged with criminal negligence. Why isn't it happening in this case?" I asked.

Finlayson couldn't answer, only saying after the inquest results they would consider it.

The inquest seemed to be the only hope. The answers would come out in that forum. Some one would be held responsible.

I called Kevin Conner at The Winnipeg Sun. Kevin was the reporter assigned to cover city hall.

I told Kevin about the discrepancy concerning the two different police reports. I also told him the city said it was my word against theirs. I had a plan. Kevin could see for himself.

I called the police department and explained to them that I would like to see the police report again. It was long and I found it difficult to read the first time as it was my son they were talking about. They agreed to let me see it again and the appointment was set for the next morning. They weren't aware that I had applied and received standing at the inquest.

I met Kevin before we went to the Public Safety Building. He read through the package that I had received from the justice department.

When we arrived at the Public Safety Building, we were met by a secretary. She had the police report in her hand and started to lead us down the hall to the same room I had been in previously.

"Is this gentleman with you, Mr. Young," she asked.

"Yes, he's a friend who came along to help," I said.

She continued to lead us down the hall. She wasn't concerned with the friend that I had brought at all.

Once in the room with the door closed, Kevin started to read. He was shocked.

"Where do I start. There's so much. I don't know where to begin," he said.

We stayed for almost two hours. Kevin took down as much of the details as possible. The names were still blacked out, but he was familiar with the titles and together we made some pretty good assumptions.

City Workers Didn't Stop Children
City employees were working next to the site

FOR MY SON

where Adam Young
was sucked into a culvert but didn't stop a group of children from playing in the spring run off, police documents suggest.

"Two employees from works and operations were unblocking culverts in the area... while a group of youths were playing in spring run off water in a drainage ditch," says a police report on the incident which is the subject of a provincial inquest.

One nearby resident quoted in the police report said a city vehicle was close to the site for most of the day.

"On the Tuesday, at any given time, there was a city truck by the manhole," Bev Fedak said in an interview yesterday.

Another resident said he warned the city the culvert was an accident waiting to happen only days before Young's death.

"When it happened, I phoned the mayor's office and said 'now are you happy - here's the death we were warning you about,'" said Paul Wereschuk.

"After the blizzard, the city never cleared the snow - we had eight-foot drifts. If the snow was removed at the time the drainage water
wouldn't have built up - it's the same story every year," said Wereschuk.

Young's father is also raising questions about an apparent discrepancy between the police report and a copy of it which is in the hands of the Justice Department.

The police report is 60 pages, but the Crown's copy is 28 pages.

"The justice department's copy of the report does not show city workers were at the site," said Rob Young.

""They (city workers) were right there the whole time. The city pulled out every reference to that in the report sent to the justice *department," claimed Young.*

The Crown attorney's office is investigating to ensure it has a complete police report prior to the inquest into Adam's death scheduled for Oct. 14-15, said Rob Finlayson, provincial head of prosecutions.

The police will compile the entire report for the Crown again, said Gord Schumacher, legal advisor for the Winnipeg Police Services.

I don't know what happened. If they're missing anything they will get it," Schumacher said.

"The city should have assumed liability and settled out of court, said Coun. Harry Lazarenko

The city cleared the snow at the culvert on April 21 - the day before Adam's death.

"Who asked for those culverts to be cleared - it was the city's responsibility," Lazarenko said.

Accusations Fly Over Partial Report
City councillors suggest cover-up

The paper trail showing who sent an incomplete police report on Adam Young's death to the Justice Department seems to have vanished - and some city councillors suggest it's a cover-up.

The Justice Department only received 28 pages of a 60 page police report about Young's death, which is the subject of a provincial inquest.

The Crown didn't receive a part of the police report that suggests city employees working in the area where Adam drowned did nothing to stop a group of children from playing in the spring run-off.

Following a story in yesterday's Winnipeg Sun, the city sent the Crown a complete copy of *the report.*

"It can't be a coincidence that all the information (originally sent to the Crown) about the city workers was excluded. It suggests an editing process," said Dave Guttman, the lawyer for Rob Young, Adam's father.

"The question is whether anyone ordered the report to be changed," said Coun. Mike O'Shaughnessy(Old Kildonan).

It's standard practice that reports don't leave the city without going through the board of commissioners, said Coun. John Prystanski (Point Douglas). No one at the board of commissioners was available for comment.

It's unfair to speculate that the oversight occurred because of a potential lawsuit against the city, said Mayor Susan Thompson.

"The police department doesn't have an explanation but the entire 60 page report has been delivered (yesterday) to the justice department," Thompson said.

Usually in criminal cases police provide the case reports. Inquests are different - I'm not sure who provided us with the (original) information in the case," Rob Finlayson, provincial head of prosecutions.

City departments also seemed baffled by the paper trail.

-The report was sent to the Crown by the police department, said Marvin Samphir, the city's senior counsel.

-It was copied and sent by a civic clerk in the police department, said Gord Schumacher, legal advisor for the Winnipeg Police Services.

-The report was delivered by the police or the civic legal department, said Tom Pearson, manager of the city's water and sewer division.

"Why would someone in police services want to be put on the hook for civic employ-

ees? What possible gain would there be? Someone was taking direction from above," said Coun. Garth Steek (River Heights).

"Civic employees don't alter reports without political direction," said Coun. Al Golden (St. Vital).

Kevin Conner, Winnipeg Sun

My main concern about the police report was the reference to city employees. Kelly Moar was using the reports, both the police and the water and waste report to compile his witness list for the inquest.

Prior to getting all these reports, Kelly had two witnesses on his list. He knew nothing of the others.

There was other city reports that had not surfaced as well.

A Works and Operations report had disappeared. The fire department report had never turned up. The Board of Commissioner's report vanished. These were the ones' I knew about. How many were around that I didn't know?

I had had the advantage of working at City Hall at the political level. I know how things operate. I know the process, afterall ,I helped create it. I know the reports that had to be written for even the most trivial incident. Everything has to be documented. After an incident like Adam's death, I found it hard to believe that the city's file consisted of only a police report and a 3 page report from the water and waste department.

With the help of Kevin, we started digging.

Some City Councillors knew we were right, and quietly directed us in our efforts.

We were told of the reports and who had written them. The city still denied their existence.

One of the best leads I received though, didn't come from the politicians.

Just days after the press released the fact that some reports were missing, a gentleman called.

"I have a picture," he said. " I was in the area and I had my camera. I saw the commotion and started taking pictures. I have pictures of the works and operations crew and the Incident Chief of the fire department. There is another photo of all of them talking and the Incident Chief is taking notes."

This proved it. There was a crew in the area. The city had denied it. There was a fire department report which they also denied and didn't send to the justice department.

He offered to give me the pictures.

"You can use these. It might help your cause," he said. I'll get them copied for you. "There's one condition. I'm a city employee and you can't mention my name. I'll get fired. They've already warned us."

> ### City Gag Order Hushes Inquest
>
> A gag order has been imposed on City employees concerning the Adam Young inquest by a top civic lawyer. The order came after it was learned the city has a second report which hasn't been forwarded to the Crown.
>
> Departments have been instructed not to discuss the case by senior city lawyer Marvin Samphir, said Jack Marquardson, spokesman for the waste and water department.
>
> Earlier this week, The Sun discovered the Justice department received only half of a police report on the incident - raising concerns of a cover-up.
>
> There is also a fire department report which is not in the hands of the Crown.
>
> "It's a standard report," said Chief Barry Lough. "It won't be forwarded unless they subpoena it," Lough said.

They won't give the justice department information unless it's subpoenaed! I was shocked.

The reports were already subpoenaed. The Justice Department asked for all information regarding the accident. Who do these people think they are? They admitted that information is missing.

How can the inquest be effective if the crown doesn't have the information needed?

I called the city legal department.

"A concerned citizen has given me pictures of the two city

workers that were on the site when Adam had died. I've given the pictures to the Winnipeg Sun and you have 24 hours to provide Kelly Moar, at the Crown Prosecutor's office with their names and the complete police report or these pictures will appear in the paper. Call Kevin Conner to confirm what I've said if you don't believe me. It's not my word against yours anymore."

Dave and I scheduled a meeting with Kelly Moar. We provided the names that we thought were necessary. Kelly agreed to subpoena our witnesses. The subpoena also stated that the witnesses had to supply the court with any reports or information that they had written or had in their possession.

Marvin Samphir's comments were that this information would be supplied at the inquest. This wouldn't give us, or the Crown, Kelly, time to review them prior to the inquest. We couldn't prepare our side without this information.

13

Dad awaits truth about boy's death
Culvert tragedy probe begins today

After five months, Rob Young is comforted by the fact that today the truth will finally come out about his son's death.

Last April, 14-year-old Adam Young was pulled into a flood-swollen culvert while he and his best friend played in pooled water near his school on Leila Avenue.

His body, which was found two weeks later, was pulled into a the city's sewer system and ended up in a catch basin at the Main Street and Armstrong Avenue lift station.

Today, a two day inquest begins into Adam's death and the circumstances around it. First on the stand will be two of Adam's friends who were playing with him near the culvert the day *he went missing.*

Also expected to testify today are a firefighter and Adam's father, Rob.

Subpoenas have been sent to at least 23 people, including two city councillors.

"What is needed now is to get the truth," said Coun. Harry Lazarenko, who is scheduled to testify. "What did happen and what could have been done to prevent this? If we could have boxed in the culverts, this may not have happened."

Young will have a lawyer asking the questions he wants answered.

"I'm pretty confident the truth is going to come out," Young said. The negligence is pretty obvious on both sides, the school division and the city.

From the day Adam's body was found, his father has been fighting for the city to identify all the open culvert sites - so far 175 have been located and repairs on them are under way.

"For four or five months it's been my word against theirs," Young said "I have no faith at all anymore. How many chances do they get?
by Kim Guttormson and Melanie Verhaeghe, Winnipeg Free Press

Dave wanted me there an hour before the court room opened. The inquest was to start at 10:00.

At 9:00, I started up to room 408. There was a crowd gathering in the hall outside the court room.

The press was there, all of them. I had been on the phone with CBC Newsworld at 7:00 that morning already. They wanted to do a live interview at noon, and they were making the arrangements. This was to be broadcast across Canada. This was becoming a national story.

Most of the other media had been following the story since the day it all began. Several reporters had become quite close and were like friends, supporters in the whole case.

Two of Adam's friends, the ones who had been subpoenaed were sitting outside the court room with their parents. I hadn't spoken to either of them since the accident.

These were two witnesses I didn't want to show up. I didn't want these kids to have to replay that day. I wanted them to forget it, get on with their lives.

I had heard that the principal of the school, Linda Paul had called all the kids that had been in the water or near it, to her office the day after the accident. She blamed them for Adam's death or at least that's what they felt like after the meeting. How could she. These kids had been through enough.

They had been friends with Adam since kindergarten, they had watched him grow up. They had attended the same elementary school together for 6 years and together they entered junior high as a group. And they had watched him die. Gary was the last person to see and touch Adam. He was the one that Adam was holding on to.

They had been through enough. Now they sat quietly in hall of the Law Courts Building. I wanted to tell them to go home.

Judge Guy entered the court room and after some preliminary introductions, Kelly Moar, representing the crown called the first witness, Justin Jones, Adam's friend.

"Justin, I understand you're thirteen years of age?" Moar asked.

"Yeah." It was an effort for Justin to get that much out.

"I also understand you attend the school, Ecole Leila North."

Justin replied, "No. I transferred to Garden City.

"Okay. On April 22 of this past year you were attending that school?"

"Yes, I was. I was attending Leila North". I could barely see Justin over the walls of the witness box, but I could see he was shaking.

Moar continued, "Perhaps you can just begin by, I understand that you were a friend of Adam Young?"

"Yes, I was."

"How long did you know him."

Justin's head went down. "Since kindergarten." I hated this. This kid should not have to be here. He shouldn't have to do this. I could tell that Kelly was uncomfortable with this too.

Kelly went on, "Perhaps just before we go into the incident itself, I take it that on April 22, at noon, you were dismissed for lunch? Do you normally remain at school to eat lunch on those days?"

"Yeah." His head was still down. He couldn't look at anybody.

"Okay, now I understand at approximately noon that day you were dismissed and proceeded to leave the school?"

"Yeah. We went and ate our lunches outside."

"And at that time were you with Adam? And approximately how many other individuals were with you?"

"About ten."

"Now, what do you recall happening."

"Well, Gary went into the water, and then Tyler followed him, like in the ditch area, near the culvert, and they were telling Adam to go in, so Adam went in, and I was playing on the snow bank near the culvert area. And then I seen - like I guess I went to get something near the culvert, and I guess Adam slipped, and I seen them trying to pull Adam up, so I ran to the fire hall, and I seen somebody running towards the school."

Kelly went on asking Justin questions about the incident and the rescue attempt that was made by the fireman. They were all surface questions.

A few weeks before the inquest, Kelly had met with Dave and I to explain his role in the proceedings. He was struggling with the fact that he was a prosecutor and was used to going for the "throat". But not in this case. All he could do was ask enough questions to reveal the facts. He wanted to do more. That was Dave's job.

Kelly questioned Justin for a total of maybe 20 minutes. Then Dave stood up.

"Justin, the day before, Gary was the only one who went in the water, is that right," Dave asked

"Yeah," Justin said. "We were watching him walk back and forth in the water.

"Did any of you, to your knowledge, tell any teachers at the school what you had been up to outside there?"

"No."

"Okay. Is it true that during the lunch hour, there is no supervision outside of the school by any of the teachers or staff?"

"The odd time there's teachers walking around with the autistic students, and the teachers watch from inside the school, in the area where the doors are, and that's about it.", Gary told the court.

There was a pause. The room was quiet.

"Okay, so for instance, if thirty or forty of you had been outside, having lunch, you would be basically unsupervised?"

"Yeah."

"Okay, one other thing. It's my understanding and you can correct me if I'm wrong, but when they dismiss you for lunch, people who want to go outside can go outside, but the school doors are locked, is that right."

Gary hesitated. "Yeah. Once you go outside, you can't come back in."

That's why the kids didn't go to the school for help. They knew the school doors were locked and the teachers and staff were inside.

The next witness was Gary Johns. Gary had also been a friend of Adam's since kindergarten. His testimony was identical to Justin's.

Gary had been playing in the water the day before. No teachers stopped him or questioned him about his wet clothes after lunch.

He confirmed that even though he had been in the ditch the day before, he didn't see the culvert inlet and there was no force or flow in the ditch. He also confirmed that there were no teachers present supervising the kids in the school yard.

During Gary's testimony, Michelle who had been sitting next to me grabbed my hand to get my attention.

"Look at him. The lawyer from the city. Look at what he's doing." she whispered.

The city had sent two lawyers from there legal department to represent them. Marvin Samphir and Kim Carswell. Samphir was the senior council for The City of Winnipeg.

And he was laughing.

Gary was on the stand, telling the court about the death of his friend. A twelve year old kid was describing a tragic accident that was unfolding right before him, and the senior counsel for the City of Winnipeg was laughing at him.

Gary described his rescue attempts and the fact that he was being sucked in and how close he was to meeting the same fate as Adam, and Samphir is laughing.

I left the court room. I couldn't sit and watch this.

The one thing I did learn, I learned outside the court room.

After Gary's testimony, I went outside the room to see if he was okay. His parents were with him, sitting on a bench in the hallway. I remembered something that both Gary and Justin had said right at the beginning of their testimony. It didn't seem important at the time.

"Gary, I didn't know that you and Justin transferred out of Leila North this year," I asked.

"Yeah, we didn't feel like going to that school anymore. Mrs. Pauls blamed us for what happened."

Gary's mother looked at me. "Rob, the whole class has gone. There's only one student left in that school from Adam's class. They've all left. The day after the accident the principal, Mrs. Pauls called the kids into her office and blamed them for what had happened. The whole class transferred out." She looked down and the three of them walked away.

14

After Justin and Gary had taken the stand, the next two witnesses were Cliff Sinclair, the acting captain of the fire hall and Dr. Joseph De Nanassy, the pathologist from the Children's Hospital.

Sinclair testified about the rescue attempt. Him and his crew of three firemen were the first on the scene. He talked about the efforts that were made to pull Gary out of the culvert opening and the attempt that his men made to search for Adam.

Dr. De Nanassy was the doctor who performed the autopsy on Adam. His testimony didn't have much of a bearing on the inquest other than to confirm that Adam had drowned in cold water.

This, he explained was different than regular drowning as there was no evidence of water in Adam's lungs. Because the water was so cold, Adam's muscles tightened to not allow water into his lungs.

I had spoken to Susan Hamilton from the Medical Examiner's office just after Adam's autopsy and she explained all this.

She also said that Adam was gone within 20 to 30 seconds of hitting water because it was so cold.

After Sinclair's and De Nanassy's time on the stand, the judge called a lunch recess. Dave headed back to his office and Michelle and I went for a walk. She was furious.

She was disgusted by the behavior of the city's lawyer, Marvin Samphir. I don't think I've ever seen her that mad or upset before.

During lunch, Michelle and I went for a walk. Nothing was really said. We both wanted to get away from the Law Courts building. The media had been there all morning and we're asking me for interviews, but nothing had really happened so far.

I was nervous about my testimony which was scheduled for the afternoon. I wasn't sure when, but I knew I would be up there.

The first witness after the lunch recess was Charles Connelly. Connelly was one of the Water and Sewer employees that was in the area. His name had been blacked out on the police report that I had seen and wasn't even forwarded to the Justice Department originally. This was one of the guys in the photograph I had received. This was one of the employees that the city had tried to hide. Why?

"Mr. Connelly, I understand that you are employed with the City of Winnipeg?" Moar started.

"Yes I am", Connelly said.

"Getting right to the point, I understand that on April 21, 1997 your crew was dispatched to the area of Leila Ave? What duties were you assigned?"

"Checking culverts, to make sure they were flowing properly."

"So you would patrol up and down Leila Ave? And you were responsible for checking all the culverts?"

"Yeah"

"And if you came upon a culvert that wasn't operating, what would you do?" Moar asked.

"Steam it out with a steamer," Connelly replied. You could tell he didn't want to say anymore than he had to.

Moar continued, "I understand on that day, April 21, you came upon a culvert that was on Leila, adjacent to the fire hall. Is that correct?"

"Yeah."

"Can you tell us what happened when you got there?"

"Well the water wasn't flowing, so we called the Sewer Department," Connelly replied. You could tell he wasn't very comfortable. He wanted to get out of here as soon as possible.

Marvin Samphir seemed to be enjoying himself, he was still laughing. At one point during Connelly's testimony, Samphir scanned the court room, then leaned over to his partner, Kim Carswell and asked, "Where's the kid's mother? Is that her?" as he pointed to Michelle. Carswell just shook her head.

Kelly continued with Connelly, "What did you actually do at that point, yourself, when you arrived at the culvert? Did you at any point attempt to unblock the culvert?"

"Yeah. We tried with the steamer, but we couldn't get through it. That's when I called the Sewer Department."

"And what happened when they got there?"

"Well, they told me to steam it again, but the steamer - we couldn't push it through with the hose, so then he sent a guy down the manhole to free the culvert. It was full of cement. Cement! Chunks of cement."

I was shocked. Dave turned around and gazed at me. Michelle squeezed my hand. Here was a hole in a school yard with enough of a suction to draw in, as Connelly said "chunks of cement". Kids played in this. Gary had been in the water the day before. This thing was dragging cement from the playground and devouring it.

Moar went on, "Was this during school hours, I assume?"

"Yeah."

"Do you remember what time it was, approximately?"

"Probably around ten, ten thirty."

"And you didn't see any children at all"

"No," Connelly replied with his head down.

Kelly continued to question Charles Connelly. The court heard how on three occasions he went back to the site to inspect the culvert to make sure it was flowing properly. Connelly also testified about the attempts that were made after he came back to the site and found out that a child had been swept away.

When Moar was finished, it was Dave's turn.

"Mr. Connelly, how many years have you been assigned to that particular area?"

"Since '91," Connelly replied as he tried several times to adjust himself in the witness box to get comfortable.

"Would you agree with me that every spring there's a large

amount of water in these particular ditches when the snow melts or is in the process of melting?"

"Not every year. Some years, there's hardly no water."

"In 1996, was there a fair amount of water?"

"Yes there was."

"And again this spring?"

"Yeah."

"I'm not sure of something, and perhaps you can clear it up for me. When you say the culvert is flowing properly, what exactly do you mean? Do you mean just the water running through. So in effect, if there isn't a bunch of water coming out onto the roadway, it appears that it's running through in a satisfactory manner?"

"Yeah."

Dave hesitated a few seconds. "You don't get out of your truck and go and check each and every one?

Connelly was silent. He looked at the judge. He turned his head and looked at Samphir. Marvin stopped smiling.

What they didn't know was I had spent a day following Connelly and his partner to see exactly what they did. They would drive by a culvert approach, slow down, and then keep going. They had no way of knowing exactly what the flow of an inlet was like.

Connelly lowered his head and mumbled, "No."

"Now would you agree with me that there was at least two and a half to three feet of water in the culvert, if you were standing in there?"

"Yeah."

Samphir wasn't smiling but Dave was.

"And you couldn't see the pipe itself?"

"No."

"Only the water above it. Is that fair," Dave asked.

"Yeah."

"Now, you would have had occasion to check back that afternoon, to make sure the problem hadn't repeated itself? And that would be done by virtue of driving by slowly and taking a look, correct?

"Right."

"You wouldn't have gotten out of your vehicle and gone over it visually?"

"No."

"And is the same thing true the following morning when you came by?"

"Yeah."

"So at that point in time, unless you came up really close, you wouldn't be able to tell the amount of the current or anything like that?"

"No."

Even though residents had been complaining about this site for some time, since the spring of 1993 to be exact, nothing was being done. This guy, whose job it is to inspect this culverts testified he doesn't even get out of his truck.

"Dave continued, "Did you have to prepare a report about the events of the previous day, on that day?"

"Yeah," he said after looking over at Marvin.

"And where is that report at this point in time? Do you have a copy with you?"

"Yeah."

Connelly leaned over and reached into his back pocket to pull out a folded piece of paper. Samphir stopped laughing again. All written reports were to be handed over to the Justice Department prior to the inquest to be used as evidence. Here was one the City neglected to hand over.

I was getting mad. So mad I had to leave the court room. I wandered the halls for the rest of Connelly's testimony. I couldn't listen to anymore. I needed a break.

Shortly after lunch, the inquest resumed.

Kelly Moar was the first to speak after Judge Guy entered the court room.

"I'm just going to call the next witness, Your Honour," Moar opened.

"Would you step into the witness box? Take the Bible in your right hand. State your name to the Court," the clerk said.

"Jean-Paul Delorme."

"Mr. Delorme, how long have you been with the Winnipeg

Fire Department?" Moar asked

"Roughly two and a half years," Delorme replied

"And how long have you been stationed at the fire station at Allan Blye?"

"I was supposed to only be there for the day. It was just a temporary change."

Moar continued, "Okay. Now, I understand on April 22nd of this year, you were in the station when a young individual came in, requesting your assistance? And do you remember what was -- what was said to you at that point?"

Jean-Paul hesitated, took a breath and then started remembering, "Well, at that point, a couple of children at the door, ringing the door bell, so Don was ahead of me. He proceeded to the door, was informed that there was a child in the culvert, and seeing that, he yelled out to me. I yelled out to my captain, stating that there was a child in the culvert. He went out. And a few minutes later -- or excuse me, a few moments later, I followed, went out of the hall, could see the child off to my right. All I could see was his head, and neck and possibly a little bit of his shoulders above the water, and Don was roughly twenty feet away from him at that time. So when I got there, Don had a firm hold of the child, and the other children in the area were stating that there was somebody
underneath him."

"Um-hum, go on."

"Not being able to see him, I stepped into the water and started doing a manual sweep, following his legs and so on. When I couldn't feel the child or anybody hanging on to him, by that time Terry Lamb had showed up, had also grabbed onto the child, and when I said, "I can't feel him," they pulled out the child."

Kelly glanced at his notes. He asked, "When you came out, you said you could see his shoulders above the water?"

"Well, maybe an inch of his shoulders just above the water."

"And today, you're unable to say which individual that was, the name?"

"I couldn't tell you his name, no."

"Okay. And at the time when you got there, one of your co-workers was already in the water?"

"He was in the water, and he had a good hold of his shoulders by that time."

"And did you get in the water at that point?"

Delorme continued, "Yeah. I crawled in. I couldn't tell if it was a manhole or a culvert. I couldn't see what we were stepping into. I slowly walked in, felt the pipe beside my leg. So then I started making -- once I heard the children saying that there was another child, that's when I started looking for the other one."

" At this point, can you describe what the water temperature was like?"

"It was extremely cold. Very cold. Yeah."

"Okay. And what about a current? Could you feel any current at all?"

"I could feel a strong draw, as if it was trying to pull my leg, which was right beside the pipe, in front of it, and even when I had a firm hold, it was pulling my arm into the culvert. Like I could feel the draw. So I made sure I had a firm hold of -- I don't know if it was the bank, but I had hold of something, and that's when I was doing my sweep. I had a hold of something. I don't know what it was. But I had some -- I couldn't see what I was holding onto. I just grabbed onto something that felt firm."

"Okay. And when you came into the water, the child was still there, the one above water?"

"Yes."

This was hard. Through out the past seven months I had avoided hearing the details. I wanted the facts not the details. I avoided reading the statements in the police report. All this was hard to hear.

Kelly continued to question the fire man.

"Okay. And are you able to state in what position he was at that point?"

"He was facing away from the culvert, with his back in the pipe. So he was arched backwards, with his back -- his back was against the pipe, and his whole -- or I'd say his bottom torso, his legs, were inside the pipe, facing backwards."

"And at this point, you indicated that it was one of your other co-workers that had a hold of him?"

"Yes. Don Shellrude had him underneath the arms, because I'd say there was about eight -- eight to ten inches of water above the pipe, and that's why you'd only see half his torso was in the pipe. The other half was -- I guess the current was pulling him, and there was -- the force was keeping him against the pipe."

"And then you indicated that you did a sweep, a manual sweep with your arm?"

"A manual sweep, yeah."

"And when you did that, what, if anything, did you feel?"

"I could feel his feet, the end of his feet, and I started doing both legs, feeling wherever I could possibly feel extra arms or anything, and I couldn't even feel his runners. His runners had been sucked off, as well. They were gone."

"That's the individual that was sitting on top?"

"The individual that was against the pipe, yeah."

"Pipe. Okay. So you couldn't feel -"

"I couldn't feel anything."

"-- Adam Young --"

"And that's when the boy himself said, "I can't feel him anymore." And so that's when we pulled him -- or the other two gentlemen pulled him out."

Gone. Just like that Adam was gone. Just like Gary's runners had been sucked off his feet, Adam was taken from us.

"And so after you made the sweep and the other individual was pulled out, Mr. Johns, what did you do then?"

"At that point, I got out of the water. They started bringing the child to the -- the fire hall. I could see my captain coming, so I went and told him, made sure that he understood that there was still a child in the pipe, that there was another child. So he radioed in to get the water rescue down. After telling him that, I went to the nearest manhole cover, pulled it out, and tried to visualize, to see if I could see the child passing or be able to see him in any way.

"I want you to take a look at this photo here. Now, the culvert that we're speaking of, do you see it in the photo here?

Moar held up a group of photographs that he had taken. It was a panoramic view of the entire area. There must have been 10 3 by 5 pictures all taped together.

"Let's see. Right here," Delorme pointed to the culvert where it all happened. You could see the school in the background and his station to right.

"Okay. Now, you indicate that's the culvert where all the

focus was?" Kelly asked

"Right."

"You said that you later went to a manhole cover. Which one would that have been?"

"Well, it was the clearest -- the closest one, so I suspect it might have been this one. I can't really tell from this photo. It might have been -- probably this manhole right here. I could guess, maybe fifty metres, I'm not quite sure. I don't know the name of this road, but it was running down this road. The first manhole cover closest to the culvert. And after pulling that one, I ran to the next one, but I couldn't remove that manhole."

"Okay. I'm just going to direct your attention to this culvert on the road. Do you recall that culvert -- culvert -- or that manhole cover, excuse me?"

"Well, that could be the one. That could be the one. I pulled up the nearest one. So that must be it. This is probably where most of the water rescue -- the vehicles were parked along this one, and I spent a lot of time near that one later on. I pulled it out with my fingers.

"Is that something normally that you could do?"

"Not normally, no."

"No. So the adrenaline was --"

"Yeah." It must have slowed down by the time I got to the second one. I couldn't remove it. I couldn't even budge it.

"Okay. Now, when you pulled the first manhole cover off, what did you do with that?" Moar asked.

You could tell this was hard for Delorme. His demeanour was getting quieter as the questioning went on.

"I pulled it aside and just started visualizing, to see if I could see the boy. All I could see was the water. The complete pipe was filled with water, and it was backwashing. There was so much water going through the pipe at that point. I could see roughly five feet down, and a big flow of water, with it hitting the back of the pipe, and flowing upwards and circling and just backwashing."

"So it was pretty turbulent?"

"There was lots of turbulence, yeah."

"And did you see anything at all?"

"Nothing."

"No?"

"Nothing."

"And then you indicate you went further down the street, further --"

"Yeah. I'd say the other pipe was maybe fifty metres away. The first one -- well, obviously only about thirty feet away."

"Okay. And that one you couldn't lift up?"

"No. I couldn't lift that one."

"And what did you do after that?"

"I stuck around, and I saw a Waterworks truck come by. I asked them if they'd be able to give us a hand, if they knew anything about what was there, if it was a culvert, pipe. I didn't know what we were working with. So he came out of his vehicle, and had a metal probe with him, and started probing the pipe to see if he could see anything. And later, after that, the chief's vehicle pulled in, and I started relaying the information to him, as to what had transpired. And not too long after that, the water rescue team showed up."

"Okay. Did you, at any point, have an occasion to observe the surface of the water culvert was?" Kelly asked.

"By the culvert?"

"Yeah?"

"As we were pulling up the child, I was looking at the boy, and as I was watching the boy, I could see basically an eddy that was circling. It would momentarily disappear, and then it would come back. And as we were doing the water rescue itself, the same thing was occurring. I was told at a later date by an engineer that due to the backwash in the pipe, the amount of flow, it was backwashing so much that it was delaying the pressure, and it would momentarily lose the eddy, and when the water started to flow again, then the eddy would come back."

"So it's safe to say that it would look at one point being calm, and then all of a sudden you'd see the eddy. Okay. And finally, when you got into the water itself, what was your footing like at that point?

"My footing wasn't too bad. It was -- there was a bit of a slope, and the fact that I
had my leg pressing against the pipe, it wasn't too, too bad."

"Okay. So you're unable to say if there's any ice on the

bottom or -- that you recall?"

"I really couldn't tell you," Delorme replied

"Good. Thank you. Nothing further."

Judge Guy looked at Moar, then reached out to grab the series of photographs

"Just before counsel ... This doesn't give us a good impression because there's no water here, but -" Guy asked Jean-Paul as he studied the pictures.

"Was there water where the -- where the manhole was, on that road there?"

Delorme looked at the pictures, then at the Judge. "How far -- like are you saying across the road, it's -- the closest manhole?"

"Yes, "asked Guy

"There might have been water coming to it, but not above the manhole."

"Okay. So -- so was it -- for example, was the road dry where that manhole cover was?"

"Where -- where you could see water farther down, if you continue down that road?" Delorme was trying to be as specific as possible.

"Yes."

"You could see water there, it went across the road there and then went back into the culvert on the other side. So it flowed across.

"Okay. But on -- but on this culvert here there was water.

"Oh, it was --"

"The way you have described it, it was covered?"

"It was roughly -- yeah, it was covered."

"Yeah."

"Now, did it go -- the water go all the way to that road?" Guy was pointing towards the school ground.

I could tell he was confused. He wanted to visualize how much water was present on that day and how close it was to the area that the kids were playing.

Delorme replied, "It went up to the road itself, touching and then it went -- where there's a low spot here, it went cross there. But here it was still dry."

"Okay. So -- so where the manhole -- cover it, it was dry?

"Yeah."

"So you could -- that's how you could --"

It was barely touching the asphalt, maybe the gravel before the asphalt."

"Because this doesn't give any depth, if I can put it that way," Judge Guy asked.

"Right."

"It looks like it's fairly --"

"Well, I was just guessing, from the size of his torso and that, there must have been eight inches of water, and maybe ten, above the culvert itself."

"Okay."

"Like we had no idea what we were dealing with because you couldn't see. You couldn't see anything."

Delorme seemed to be justifying himself and his actions.

A few days after the accident, I had spoken to Captain Sinclair from the fire station. He told me that the men from his station that tried to help were shaken by the events that had taken place. In almost all the incidents that firemen attend, when they leave, their job is over and things are under control. Not this time. When they left the scene, Adam was still in there. There job didn't seem finished. They had a hard time leaving this scene.

And the fact that it was almost in their own backyard didn't help. They felt like failures. And that feeling came back every time they looked out their window.

"And -- and this culvert goes under -- under -- and perhaps someone else will ask this, but the culvert goes under this road."

"Correct," Delorme answered.

Guy continued, "and then, when you say you looked down in this manhole you saw five or six feet where the water from the culvert was going in?

"Right."

"Okay."

"It's as if it was a big empty tube. Down about five feet below you could see the water and it was going -- you could see the hole itself, but it was -- the backflow, it would go up roughly three feet high from the water hitting and backflowing."

Guy studied the set of pictures, seemly unaware of the crowded court room. After a few moments he looked at Dave.

" Mr. Guttman?" Guy stated.

Dave stood up from the table and placed his hands in his pockets.

"Yes, Your Honour. Thank you. Mr. Delorme, I take it that you had occasion to speak with your co-workers after this somewhat hair-raising incident? Did they tell you how much force they had to use in order to lift this one boy out of the water?"

Delorme looked at Guttman then at the Judge, "Well, roughly, they were saying that Don had him by the arms. The other gentleman was pulling him on the legs, one leg at a time, in order to be able to pull him out of that -- that pipe."

"These are pretty strong gentlemen, aren't they?"

"I would say so."

"Okay. Is it fair to say that if you and your co-workers had not got there at the time that you did, that maybe we'd be dealing with more than one individual passing on?

"I would think so, yes. I'd say another minute or so he would have been cold enough that he wouldn't have been able to hang on anymore."

"You've had occasion now to see a photograph in front of you there with the culvert without water in the ditch that is next to it. Would you agree with me that if there was a cover on that pipe, probably nothing tragic would have taken place on -- on April 22nd, other than boys playing in the water?"

Jean Paul looked again at Guttman, and then stared at Samphir who was smiling.

"True, yeah. If -- if the pipe would have been blocked off, there was no way the boy would have been able to have been drawn into it in such a way.

"And you spoke of a strong draw, to use your words. Have you swum in a lake or the ocean where there is a current that drags you?" Dave asked.

"Not really, no."

"No. So you don't have a basis upon which to gauge the degree of current here?"

"I couldn't tell you how strong. I could just relate that if I would have had my leg in front of it, it would have pulled it in somewhat."

"And you made every effort you could to try and feel for the boy underneath?"

"Basically, I couldn't feel him. I went right to the end of his feet, and not being able to go any farther into the pipe, like I couldn't feel -- like when you can feel his toes and feel no shoes on him, you could pretty well relate that there was nothing hanging on to him."

"When you pulled this manhole off, I assume that when you were talking about a backwash effect, could you see that where the pipe empties in, it's on a downward angle? Could you see that?"

"I couldn't tell you if it was at an angle or not. All you could see was basically the top of the pipe, the water striking the cement above it, because there was more water than can flow into the pipe, and it would simply roll. It would hit, fly up maybe three feet and then fall back into the pipe."

Dave stood quietly with his hands in his pockets. He turned to look at me then asked, "Do you recall if the boy that was rescued still had his shoes at the time he was taken out of the water?"

"No, he didn't have his shoes on."

"So they went down the pipe, presumably?" Dave asked

Delorme stared at no one. "They went down the pipe, as well."

"We heard earlier testimony from your acting captain. I'm just wondering if you can give us an idea of what the distance was from where the manhole cover is to the top of the water level, as you saw it there?"

"You're talking the first manhole in the culvert? Like I say, from this photo, I would relate that it might be just coming up to the gravel. So that water lying across, but it wasn't on the asphalt. It was coming to this low spot here. There, was water on the road.

"I'm saying when you actually look inside the manhole, how close is the water? If you put your hand in there how long would it have taken --"

"You had to crawl into the pipe. There's handrails. You might have to go down four or five rungs. So you had maybe four or five feet, for sure, before you would hit water."

"And you obviously couldn't see the boy --"

"I couldn't see the boy, no," Delorme's head lowered

"When you -- you looked in there?"

"No."

"And my understanding is your orders were not to proceed downwards until the appropriate equipment was present?"

"Exactly," Delorme justified.

"Did you feel the effects of having been in the water for that short period of time because of how cold it was?

"Well, I was shivering. I later had the flu. For the next three days I was ill, after the fact.

"I thank you. Those are my questions."

Dave sat down. His points were made.

Judge Guy looked at table towards the City's lawyers

"Mr. Samphir, any questions?

Samphir smiled, "I have no questions."

"Fine. Thank you."

Guy shook his head and mumbled something to himself.

"Thank you. You are excused," he said to Jean-Paul.

15

"It's the Crown's intention at this time, Your Honour, to call Mr. Young."

It was my turn. Kelly and Dave had planned this. Usually at an inquest, the family is the last to take the stand. They wanted to leave the judge with the a sense of loss. They wanted him to feel sympathy for the family, to try and understand what we were going through.

But this was different. Because I knew so much, and had done so much of the investigative work, Kelly and Dave wanted me there now. They wanted me to lay it all out and then let the city and the school division defend themselves against what I had uncovered.

"Mr. Young, you and I have talked on quite a few occasions about this -- this incident. You've heard a lot of testimony this morning about Adam Young who we understand is your son. Perhaps if you would, sir, if you would begin, if you can just tell us who your son was?"

I started to shake. Over time, I managed to separate the fact that this accident happened to my son. I had to do this to keep focused. To keep doing what had to be done.

"I don't know what to -- how to start. He was my oldest son. He had been out sandbagging along Scotia Street, helping people out. That's -- that's what he was like. And he was a black belt in karate, had all the levels of swimming that you can get. He ..." What do you say. He wants to know who Adam was. He was my son, isn't that enough.

I started to cry.

"Sorry," I apologized. To this day, I don't know why I had to apologize to anyone for anything.

"I understand he was the oldest of your three children? Your other children were -- are how old?"

"Twelve and nine," I answered.

"And your son had been attending the school, Ecole Leila North, for how long?"

"This was his second year. He -- he didn't want to go to that school, but he went."

I remembered the conversation Adam and I had about a year earlier. He wanted to switch schools. I talked him out of it, telling him to stick it out. Maybe he knew something then.

Kelly continued, "You heard testimony earlier today from some of the other children, that your son had been playing inside the water in question. Had you been aware of that at all?"

"No. I didn't know he had been -- that they had been playing in it or -- or they were intending to. It doesn't surprise me. Adam liked water. He was drawn to it, like a lot of other kids are."

"Also, as you're aware of, I spoke with your -- with your wife with respect to this matter, and she has asked that you actually relay her thoughts through you, she didn't want to appear today."

"Yes. She can't. He was not only a son. He was a friend. He was that kind of kid that every year, if there were toys that he didn't want, he would clean them up and take them to the Cheer Board or donate them someplace, and just always wanted to be involved.

"He was very involved in his church and never got into fights. I mean even though he -- he had a high level in karate, he -- he refused to use it, to the point where last year he stayed home for a week because there was some kids bugging him, and he just refused to get involved in anything like that," I said.

I thought for a few moments then said, "I'd like to say he was a good student, but he was a teenager, he wasn't. He didn't ..."

"Now, my understanding is that your son, once he left home in the morning, would stay at school all day?"

"Yeah."

"He'd eat his lunch at school?"

"Yeah."

"And what were the arrangements during the day for him?" Kelly asked.

"He would, him and Kevin would walk to school, right by that spot, because most of the kids from that area, that's how they come, from the north side. They would walk right by it, and they would stay at school for lunch and then come home at 3:30."

Now Kevin was going to have to walk by himself. Walk right by that spot. Twice a day, five days a week.

"And what was your understanding of the arrangements during the lunch hour, for your son?" Moar asked.

"That they stayed at school and that they were supervised."

Kelly stopped and stared at his notes. He flipped a few pages over. "Okay. Now, it's fairly obvious, once the incident occurred and subsequent, that you became very involved in trying to find out what happened to your son."

"Yeah."

"Do you want to comment on that aspect?"

I looked over at Dave then at Samphir. Marvin had his pen ready. I could tell he was getting his ammunition ready. I had embarrassed them in the press, with the public and he was going to get me.

"I don't know where to start. The day after the accident -- maybe I'll go back. I used to be the executive assistant to several City Councillors, one of them from that area, so I know them quite well, and Councillor O'Shaughnessy called me in the morning and said, "Is there anything I can do?" And I asked him to -- to make sure that this doesn't happen again and to give me details on what the chances are they would find him, because they still hadn't found him at that point. So he took me to the Works and Operations building, and we met with the Director of Water and Waste. And they assured me that regardless of the cost and regardless of what the Legal Department said, these things would be fixed."

Kelly wanted clarification. "These things, meaning?"

"These culverts. It just didn't happen. They didn't -- they stuck a piece of chain-link fence in the hole and thought that was appropriate," I said. "Since then I've found -- I've personally found six like this, that are near day cares or elementary schools, and have reported it to the City, but nothing is done. I waited 'til July, and still no response, so I took it upon myself -- Kevin, my twelve year-old, and I fixed this particular culvert so it won't happen again."

"What did you do to fix it?"

"I drilled a hole on each side of the culvert and put a piece of re-bar through it, and I know that the City is concerned that garbage is going to get stuck in there, so I drilled two holes, and put pins in it, so that they can pull the bar out, clean the debris out and then put the bar back in. I've contacted every province in Canada, through their Attorney General's Department, asking if there have been similar incidents like this. I've -- they have responded back, and the only incident that has happened was in 1984, in Calgary. Within three months after the child died, all the culverts were covered with some form of bars."

I stopped to take a breath. The grief was subsiding.

"Two miles north of where this site is," I said, "is East St. Paul, and they are all covered. Winnipeg is the only city in Canada that does not have them covered.

"When you heard that the inquest was called into the death of Adam, what were you hoping would happen as a result of this inquest?" Kelly asked.

"I was hoping that the threat of an inquest would be enough to make somebody do something. If you remember, around the same period, a five year-old boy crawled into a Dickie Dee ice cream cart and he suffocated, and from what I understand of the medical examiner's office, that they take a six or eight week period, and they look at all the deaths that have happened, and that's how they determine if there should be an inquest or not. So this child's death was at the same time -- or within a few weeks of when Adam died, but the corporation that built these things acknowledged that they had made a mistake, their equipment was faulty and that they would do whatever it took to make sure that this didn't happen again, by building safety latches inside there, so the medical examiner did not require an inquest in this because this company had come forward," I said.

Marvin wasn't smiling now. "But with respect to this, the medical examiner was sent inaccurate information, drawings that weren't accurate, of the situation. I was told that if Adam had of been a strong swimmer, he would have been able to save himself, but because he was a weak child, that's why he died."

"I was -- like I said earlier, I was promised that these things would be fixed, on April 23rd. Nothing. I was told a couple of weeks later it would be fixed. Still nothing. Then I was told of an engineer's report, or a report that they had ordered through a particular company, and they were waiting for the results of this report. I had two people phone this company and ask them what the status of the report was. They knew nothing of a report that was ordered." I was starting to get mad.

"The Chairman of Works and Operations stood up in council, and said that the report was finished and that he had read it. This was at the council meeting in September, on September 24th. But the next day, according to the Commissioner of Works and Operations, this report was not finished."

"When I was -- when I asked for information on what had happened, or details of land drainage systems, I was told no, because of a potential lawsuit."

"I spoke to several civil engineers across Canada. I tried to speak to the fellows at the University of Manitoba and was told that they would not speak to me because they knew all the engineers at the City of Winnipeg and they risked their reputation," I said. It seemed like this was the first time I was talking about all this. I knew it wasn't, I had been telling this story all along. But now it seemed like everyone was listening.

"I spoke to a civil engineer in Toronto, who asked me details about the site, and he came back and said that the force at the end of that culvert was enough to suck in somebody who was two hundred pounds. Adam was not a small boy. He was about a hundred and fifty pounds. And you have heard the Fire Department personnel talk about the force of that water, but yet they don't seem to want to do anything about it."

"The school division does not want to supervise children.

They have told me that children are not their responsibility. They will not be supervising children."

"I understand why this site is like this, because they don't have enough development in the area to warrant a proper drainage system, but it doesn't help when the City -- I don't want to say forces, but convinces the developers in that area to sell this land for a dollar to the school division because then there is no tax base to build a proper drainage system. There is no money available to develop it, so until there is further development in this area, the residents of this area will have to live with this situation."

Finally Kelly stepped in. He asked, "Prior to the incident with your son occurring, were you aware of any concerns expressed of this area, i.e., danger for the children?"

"In August of 1993, while I was employed as the executive assistant to the Councillor of that area, yes, there was three people on that street that phoned about the amount of water that was there. I went and visited one particular person who lives on the corner of Leila and Manila. I can't recall his name. I've tried to get in touch with him, but I understand he doesn't live there anymore, to show me the damage to his yard and his basement, yes."

"Since the accident, I've had three people come forward and say that they had made complaints prior to this. One person -- sorry, two people had filed a claim with the City of Winnipeg a week prior to the accident." Marvin wasn't smiling but he was taking notes.

"One of the women, Mrs. Feduk, who works nights, came home Monday -- or Tuesday morning, from work, and could hear the water flowing from her back yard, and she said it sounded like rapids, and she warned her children to stay away, but unfortunately she did not make a formal complaint."

"When you say heard water running like rapids, where was that from?" Kelly asked.

"Where was it from? From in her back yard, because she -- there's a back lane there, and that's where they park, when she came home from work Tuesday morning."

"She was standing there when she heard it?"

"Yeah."

Kelly continued with his questions, "And where was this water running from, though?"

"This was from the culvert on the street," I said.

"That we're speaking of, where your --." Kelly couldn't finish his question, but I knew what he was asking.

I lowered my head. "Yeah."

"Okay. Now, these complaints that you speak of that were filed, were they complaints of high water levels, or complaints of children playing in water? Are you aware of that at all?"

"According to Mr. Wereschuk, there were complaints about the high water levels. He had phoned the Mayor's office the day before the accident and said, "What's it going to take? Someone to die before you do something?" He had tried to contact people all week -- all weekend. I understand one City Councillor was at the site two days before the accident, to see what it was like, but still nothing was done."

"The school division had been warned about supervising children, but still they did not do that."

"Are you aware of any instances or," Kelly asked, " in prior years, where the school division actually did supervise children? Was that actually in place?"

"No."

"No?"

"No."

"So it's never been a situation where, as far as you know."

I interrupted Kelly, "That they'd supervise children?"

"Yeah. During the lunch hour?"

"No. We had -- there's been parents -- since the accident and prior to, actually, there's been parents that I've spoken to about the fact of supervision. I know there was problems with -- with Adam and his younger brother, Kevin, about a group of kids picking on them, and the principal, at that time, refused to do anything, so we had to keep them home for a week until things calmed down. Seven Oaks does not have a violence policy, so they would not deal with it."

"Over the past two years, twenty-three children have transferred out of that school. In fact, the City Councillor for that area has taken his daughter out of that school."

Mike had taken his daughter out of Leila North the year before because of problems with the principle. She was attending a private school for girls.

I continued, "According to the school division, children are not their responsibility."

"What do you mean by that?"

"They will not supervise them. They won't -- I -- I've heard of -- and I haven't seen it, but I've heard of instances where children are getting beat up and the teachers are standing there watching, from the door." This change in supervision policy occurred when the school division changed to the middle school system. The age group attending middle schools is as young as 11 years old to a high of 16. It is against the child welfare act to leave an 11 year old alone in your home, but yet the school system is allowed to leave 11 year olds unattended at school.

Moar asked, "Is it safe to say that much of the information you have relayed is from investigation or inquiries you have made yourself with other individuals?"

"A lot of it has been, yeah. I ran for school trustee in that area, so I was aware of a lot of the problems, which is one of the reasons why I ran," I said.

"Finally," Kelly asked, "I just want to ask you is, what would you like to see happen, ultimately?"

"I want to see these -- these things fixed, and I want to see supervision for children at all schools. I know this isn't the only school that's going through this right now."

"Do you feel if those things were in place, that this tragedy could have been avoided?"

"Definitely."

The court room was quiet. Kelly stared at his notes, then looked to Judge Guy, "Nothing further, Your Honour."

Guy looked over at Dave, "Mr. Guttman, have you any ..."

The judge didn't need to finish his request. Dave was ready to go. He wanted to start.

We had talked about what could happen in court during the inquest. He described Judge Guy as "no nonsense". He would not tolerate much. This is why both Dave and I applied for standing at the inquest. If one of us was removed from the room, the other could continue.

"Mr. Young, I'm showing you a photograph. Can you tell me if you are familiar with that photograph?"

"Yes."

"Did you take this photograph?"

"Yeah."

"In May of 1997?" Dave asked

"Yeah."

"Can you describe to His Honour what it is?"

"It's a culvert similar to the one where Adam died. It's -- it's a bit bigger in -- in diameter. It's on the corner of Roblin and Harstone. And it has grates on it," I said

Dave continued, " I'd like to tender that as an exhibit, Your Honour.

Judge Guy reached for the picture. "I believe that's Exhibit 10. Thank you."

"Now, Mr. Young, in addition to all of the efforts you have made to date, did you also make requests of the City, in terms of access to information, to see reports?"

"Yes, on several occasions." I had requested all the reports both verbally and through the Access to Information Act.

"And what happened as a result of that?" Dave asked.

"Well, people's first reaction was -- to me, anyways, was, Are you going to file a lawsuit? And I said no, I was not going to. All I wanted was to see these things fixed. I went -- I did a press conference with the Mayor and stated that publicly. This is not the time for a lawsuit, it's the time to, first of all, find him, and make sure this doesn't happen again."

"I approached the City as working together to make sure that these -- this didn't happen, by let's come up with something to fix it. But every time I asked for information, I was denied because of a potential lawsuit. I went through the official Access to Information Act and was denied because of a potential lawsuit."

He continued questioning, "Did you speak with an individual named Wayne Benedet, in an effort to design an appropriate cover for these types of pipes that have been referred to as culverts?"

"Yeah. Mr. Benedet is an engineer. He had concerns about this situation for a number of years. The day after the accident -- actually, the night of the accident, he was so upset, he sat down and drew up plans for a cover, and faxed them to the City Councillor the next morning."

"My understanding is that was done in late April. Has there been any action in regard to that?"

"Nothing."

"Have you been in touch with Mr. Benedit since?"

"Yes."

"You spoke earlier about the City providing inaccurate information to the office of the medical examiner. Can you tell His Honour what you are referring to?"

"I'm referring to a letter dated June 11th, I think, that was accompanied with a drawing."

Dave seemed to taken Marvin's smile. "And is it the drawing, in particular, that causes you difficulty?"

"It's the whole document," I said.

"Perhaps you'd like to take it and advise His Honour exactly what creates the difficulties for you."

"First of all, the difficulty I have is that this is the death of somebody. This is the Department of Justice asking for official documentation on what happened. The second paragraph of this report says, "The culvert opening was approximately fourteen inches. They did not even take the time to go and measure it. And this is two and a half months after the accident."

I continued reading from the letter, "the third paragraph, "In our experience, this type of installation is not a hazard to the public."

"Even after somebody has died, they still won't admit that these are dangerous."

"On page 2, "Immediately after the accident, the culvert at Leila, where Adam Young was drawn into, was covered with chain-link fencing and barricaded."

"We've already presented the photograph of what they did. They stuck a piece of chain link fence in the hole. That opening is still big enough to draw somebody in because I stood in there."

"A directive was subsequently issued to field staff who maintain the land drainage system to locate and make secure any similar installations."

"This letter was dated June 11th. On June 18th, the person who reports to the fellow who wrote this was not aware of any directive, and his quote was, "We don't have people out looking for these sites. We are behind in other projects."

"It goes on to say that a review will be completed by the end of June, 1997. We're now into October. There's -- as far as I know, there's still no review."

"Standard construction drawings will be developed for the purpose within next one month period."

"Which means that they should have been done by July. Still nothing. The drawing that they sent with this document shows the water level at about six inch -- six or seven inches into the ditch. It shows the pipe running parallel to the ground. It doesn't. It flows at an angle. I've used the analogy that this is like a water slide. It shows a large enough air space that -- and I can see why they would say if Adam was a strong kid, he could have saved himself. But we've heard testimony that the water was about a foot from the top of the manhole cover."

Judge Guy looked at Dave, "Do you wish that filed as an exhibit?"

"Yes." Dave replied. "I would like that to be Exhibit 11."

"Now, it's my understanding, Mr. Young, that as somebody who understands the workings of city council, having been an executive assistant, you took it upon yourself to speak with a number of Councillors about this issue that's become extremely important to you; is that fair?"

"Yeah."

"And to your knowledge, a number of them have made efforts, as well? And yet, still nothing has been done, to your knowledge, other than this chain-link fencing being put at this particular site?"

"Unfortunately, the politicians do not have the power to do anything, and I'm taking that from my experience at city hall. I'm also taking that by the comment that was made to me July 23rd, the day -- or April 23rd, the day after the accident, that regardless of what the Legal Department says, we will fix these things. I was told by a City Councillor that the City will not be fixing them because they are showing liability."

"And your concern is that if something isn't done and done before next spring, this could happen again and it could happen more than once, to other people's children, as well?"

"There are a hundred and seventy-five of these that are located near schools and day cares in Winnipeg, yeah."

"Those are my questions."

We'd made our point. Now the city and the school had to

defend against what I had laid out.

Judge Guy asked, "Mr. Samphir, any questions?"

Samphir had been quiet so far. He hadn't cross examined anyone to this point, but we knew this would change now.

Samphir stood, "I wonder if we just can have a few minutes to take a look at some of the new exhibits that were filed?"

"Okay." Guy stood up and left the court room through the back door.

"Let's talk," Dave motioned for me to leave the court room. "Let's go down here."

We found a small interview room off the main hallway.

"You're doing great, but Samphir's going to try and get you. You've dumped a lot in there. They look pretty bad and he has to try and get you," he said.

"He can't do a thing. I've got all the paper work to justify everything I said," I told him.

"He has too. The city sent him to represent them and he hasn't said anything. He hasn't questioned any witnesses. He's saving it for you. You've embarrassed them in the press and now in court. He has to do something," Dave said.

He didn't seem concerned. It was like he was coaching his star player. He was pumping me up.

After the short recess, we entered the court room. I went directly to the witness box. Judge Guy entered the court and motioned to Samphir, who was smiling.

"Mr. Young, perhaps you can just clarify something for me, if you would. You said that within a day after the accident on April 22nd, you had a meeting with people at the City?" Marvin was looking at his notes and smiling.

"Yes." That was it. There is no way I'm going to have a conversation with this guy. If he wants anything from me, he's going to have to work at it.

"Who did you meet with that day?"

"Councillor O'Shaughnessy and Tom Pearson." Short and to the point.

"And who was it that told you that you wouldn't get any information even if the law department suggested that you shouldn't be able to get information?"

"That's not what I said." It was hard not to yell.

Dave jumped, "Your Honour, I don't believe that was his evidence."

"Okay okay," Marvin said putting his hands in the air.

"I believe his evidence was that came much later. I think that meeting was to assure him that things were -- were going to be done," Dave demanded.

"Well, if my note is wrong, then I apologize," Samphir said.

Judge Guy looked at Samphir in disgust, " I don't think we heard anything with respect to the gist of that meeting on the first occasion."

How could this guy do this. His organization was responsible for the death of my son and he was going to try and embarrass me in a court of law. For my sake this was the best thing he could have done. I was on the edge. He wasn't going to get me.

"Well," Samphir said as he looked down at his notes. "Maybe I ran it with another day. I apologize. Maybe it's in the wrong order. Sorry."

Strike one!

"So at that meeting, you weren't told that, just to make -- sorry about the confusion." He was trying to regain his composure.

"I was told what, sir?" No way. If you want it, work for it.

"At what meeting -- when were you then told you wouldn't get any information because that -- because of a potential lawsuit?" He was trying to throw me.

"There was no meeting. I received letters back from various departments of the City of Winnipeg," I said as calmly as I could. "And you were carbon copied those letters, sir."

"So you're talking about your request for information under the Access to Information Act?"

"I'm talking about that. I'm talking about going to Works and Operations on May 6th, I think it was, and speaking to Mr. Pearson. He told me that he would forward the information to me as soon as possible. I received a letter back from him in June, I think saying that I would not get any information because of a lawsuit, and he would forward that information to my solicitor, which has never happened. But you should have a copy of that because all these letters were carbon copied to you."

"Oh, he would forward the information to your solicitor?"

"Yes. Yes."

He paused. "Okay. So you're talking about May and June. You were given access, were you not, or you were allowed to read the police report?"

"The original police report, yes, I was, but the names were blacked out."

"Yes. But you were allowed to read the complete police report?"

"Yes."

"And you made the comment, just so that we can better understand your evidence -- or someone made the comment to you, "We will fix -- we will fix it, no matter what the cost and what legal -- what the Legal Department says." That's how I interpret your question -- your suggestion," Samphir asked.

Judge Guy glared at Marvin, "That was the response!"

"And the question I ask, who said this and when? Who said that to you?"

I didn't want to look at him. I stared straight ahead and said, "That was on April 23rd, at 10:30 in the morning, in Mr. Pearson's office, at Works and Operations."

"So that was in April?"

"Yes, that was the day after the accident."

"That it -- oh, so --"

"I was told these will be fixed, regardless of the cost and regardless of what the Legal Department says."

"Okay. So that was made to you by Mr. Pearson then, that day?"

"I can't remember if it was Mr. Pearson or O'Shaughnessy. It was a difficult time and I can't recall who said that."

Samphir paused again. He knew what had happened in that meeting. His department met the night of the accident to discuss their liability. When incidents like this happen, the organization is supposed to "circle the wagons", close up and protect themselves, not have private meetings and make promises like the one I was given. But because I used to be in this group, O'Shaughnessy wanted to help. His gesture of having this meeting was legitimate, it was a human response to a tragedy. But it was not what the legal department wanted. At the time they didn't know this meeting was taking place. In their circle, you don't do that.

Marvin lost again. He had to change the subject.

"Okay. I just," he didn't know where to go, " -- now, you -- you also said that in July you -- you fixed the culvert on your own?"

"With my twelve-year old son, yes," I said.

"Yeah. The reason why I'm going to ask you this question is that my understanding is that as you have indicated in filing what I think is Exhibit 9, just to refresh your -- the City initially put the chicken wire fence around the culvert itself, and then also had this other fenced off area, which is a snow fence?"

"Right. But that was down by the end of May."

"Okay. But that was initially there?"

"That was also taken down at the end of May."

"Well, I understand what," Samphir was grinning. "Because that's what I was going to ask you. I understand when it was taken down in May, that what the City did, was they put two re-bar -- two pieces of re-bar, in an X -- almost in an X-shape across the culvert, and that, I understand, was put in prior to your putting in the re-bar that runs parallel to the ground?"

"No, sir, it was not."

"So it's your evidence that was not there?"

"The bar that I put in there was the only bar that was on that culvert the first week of July." Now he was trying to take credit for what Kevin and I did.

"Okay. I'll tender this as Exhibit "A", just for Identification, because we'll be calling on --." He handed the judge four photographs, turning them so I couldn't see them from the witness box.

As I watched Samphir approach the Judge Guy's bench I said, "What I did do, was three days after I had installed that bar, I had a friend of mine, in that area, go and look to make sure it was still there. He confirmed that it was there and that somebody else had come along and put two more pieces in."

Samphir turned to me and stared. He didn't expect that. He didn't think I was smart enough to get a witness to this. But I did, and Tim was in the court room ready to confirm my story.

Strike three!

He had to change the subject again.

"I see. And you said you -- you got -- you have information that Winnipeg is the only city in Canada that doesn't cover culverts?" he asked.

FOR MY SON

"That I'm aware of, yes."

"And you have copies of that information or a list of the cities where -- where culverts the size of the one which we are speaking of are all covered?"

"Not in my possession at this time, no." Dave had warned me prior to the start of the inquest, that the City wanted the information that I had. I had a fairly thick file of evidence that I had gathered over time.

"Give me the file. When they ask you for it just say "It's not in my possession at this time," Dave said early that morning.

Marvin went on, "And is that the policy, as you understand it, or is that actually a copy of some written information you received from these other cities? Because it would be helpful to know what other -- what the policies in other cities are, if that's available?"

"It's based on telephone conversations I've had. It's also based on the Inquiries -- Fatal Inquiries Act report that was filed in 1984, from Calgary."

"Oh, I see."

"And also Edmonton. And just observations made on my -- by myself, driving around."

"I see."

"West St. Paul, East St. Paul, St. Anne's."

He wasn't winning this one so Samphir changed the subject again, "Now, you said that you had -- that some -- that an engineer by the name of Wayne Benedit or Benedet, I'm not sure if that's the right pronouncing.

"Wayne Benedet, yes."

"Made available to someone at the City, I think you said it was a Councillor, a -- a design for a cover?"

"Yeah. It's a design for a -- not necessarily a cover. It's bars that go overtop of the opening. And on the -- one of the bars, there is a place to put a warning sign."

"Do you know which Councillor that was given to, and do you have a copy of what was provided?"

"It was faxed to Councillor O'Shaughnessy, who has forwarded it on to Mr. Pearson, at Works and Operations, and that was done on April 24th, and it was forwarded to Mr. Pearson on April 26th." I had names and exact dates. I had the entire paper trail on this one. Someone forgot to circle the wagons on this.

"And when you said that there are Councillors who said that they can't fix the culvert and if I look in this picture, and if the information I have is correct, that in fact they put these two pieces of re-bar across, which is fixing --,"

He was trying to credit again. "I'm not sure who fixed that," I said.

"No, just if -- if my information is correct, that the City did that?"

"That's your information, sir. Not the truth."

"When were you told about the -- that the City can't fix the culvert because of possible legal liability, if they admitted that there was a problem with the culvert?"

"This was at the beginning of September, in the minutes of the Works and Operations meeting, the in-camera meeting, dated September 13th."

"Were you present at that meeting, or --," he knew that 'in-camera' means private, closed to the public and the minutes are sealed from city staff and the public.

"No," I said.

Marvin was smiling. He thought he was going to get me on this one. "-- or just from notes from the meeting?"

"From one of the people who was present at that meeting."

"Oh." The smile dropped. He paused, almost afraid to ask. "Who was the person who told you that?"

"Councillor Lazarenko."

For whatever reason, I looked over at the other city lawyer, Kim Carswell. Her head was down.

"And when were you told that?" Marvin asked.

"It was about a week after the meeting."

"And yet you -- you said that your friend who went out and checked the culvert in July, I think you told me --July. Just after you put in the bar yourself, said that someone had put in these crossbars?"

"Right, someone. But nothing has been done with the six other ones that I've reported."

"Well, I was just going to ask you there, who -- when you say you reported things, who did you report them to? Again Mr. Pearson or --"

I replied, "Mr. Pearson went on MTN News about a month

ago and warned people not to fix these things themselves, and gave a phone number to call if citizens had concerns about open culverts, that if they made the information available to the City, they would come out immediately and fix them."

"And so you phoned in six locations?"

"Yes."

"In September?"

"Yes."

"And you have since checked them and they are not fixed, at least --"

"Right." I had driven by three of them the day before.

"Do you have a list of those?"

"I can make available a list. Offhand, there is one on the corner of Markham and Waverley, about ten feet from a day care. There is three of them, Grant and Haney, next-door to Royal elementary school, that catches the runoff from the -- the golf course."

"Is that on the golf course or in the city property?"

"It's in city property, in the ditch."

"And when you say there's a hundred and seventy-five of these near schools, et cetera, by "these", you mean culverts the size of this one which is by the school on --

"No. I mean culverts that lead directly into the storm sewer or sanitation sewer system, I replied. I could see what he was implying. That the size of the opening was the issue. It wasn't. The issue is the design and the locations of the inlets.

"Is that information you received from someone else or is that your own --."

"Yes."

"I see. And when you say information from someone else, who is that information from?"

"Tom Pearson, the Director of Water and Waste."

"Oh, so you're going by what -- you're -- you're then relying on recent statements made by his department, that there has been a consultant looking into this matter and they have identified a hundred and seventy-five culverts that require some attention?"

"Right. On April 23rd, when I met with Mr. Pearson and Councillor O'Shaughnessy, he told me at that time that there was approximately a hundred and ten."

"But in any event, the -- the number one seventy-five is the recent information that's been released by Mr. Pearson's department?"

"Yes."

"As a result of his having received information from a consultant, and you know that?" Now Marvin was getting mad.

"According to Mr. Pearson's letter to the medical examiner, they were going to do a land drainage database search to find out how many there were. I don't know if there was -- this is from the consultant's report."

"Okay. Now, you say that there was a call to the Mayor's office made by, I believe it would be Mr. Wereschuk, although I could -- could be wrong, where he suggests how long -- does something -- someone have to die, or words to that effect, before this is fixed?"

"Um-hum." He was changing direction again.

"When was that call made; did he tell you?"

"That was made the Monday prior to the accident."

"The Monday prior to the accident?"

"The accident happened on a Tuesday. It was made the Monday, yeah." Paul Wereschuk had provided me with a detailed synopsis of everything that had transpired on those days.

"Oh, I see. So we're talking about April 21st '97. Did he tell you who he spoke to in the Mayor's office?"

"No. But I've spoken to the person that he spoke to." I guessed on this one.

"Well, who did you speak to?"

"His name is Ken." Ken is the receptionist in Mayor Thompson's office. I assumed he was the one who took the call.

"Ken who?"

"I'm not sure of his last name."

"So you spoke to Ken?"

"Um-hum." I had spoken to Ken on several occasions.

"In the Mayor's office. Do you know if Mr. Wereschuk made any other complaints to the City."

"He phoned on several occasions."

"And did he tell you that his complaints were related to run-off that was flowing into his yard and basement?"

"I'm -- I'm not sure I follow what you're saying."

"Well, did he tell you -- did he complain to you -- did he tell you he was complaining about flooding to his property?"

"He was complaining about flooding to the property and the excess amount of water that was in the area, yes."

"All right. And you will agree with me that just prior to the twenty -- well, in close proximity to the 21st of April, there was a severe snow storm in Winnipeg?"

"Yeah. And I also know that the City of Winnipeg did not clear that site of snow. They dumped more snow on that site." He had tried everything to shift the blame. Now he was going to use the snow storm that happened weeks before.

"Well, again this is information that you gained from where?"

"From seeing it."

"From seeing it?" he asked.

"My children still live in that area, and I drive by that area all the time. I also testified here or there that my two sons did walk by that spot every day, to go to school, to and from."

He should have quit sooner. After strike three he should have left the plate.

Samphir hung his head. "Those are the questions, Your Honour," he said quietly.

Judge Guy looked up. "Thank you. I'll allow you at the end, Mr. Guttman, if Mr. Young wishes to speak to you later, if you wish to make a closing statement of some sort, and if anything he wishes to say comes to him in the meantime, you can include that at that time."

Dave smiled, "Certainly."

"Thank you, Mr. Young. You can have a seat, " Guy said.

16

"We have one final witness for today, Your Honour, Mr. Wereschuk. I'll just call him in." Kelly said to Judge Guy.

Paul Wereschuk. Paul lives across the street from the culvert where Adam had died. He was one witness that the City didn't want called.

The court clerk stood and faced Paul. "Would you just stand in the witness box and take the Bible in your right hand? State your name to the Court."

"Paul Wereschuk."

"Thank you. You may be seated," she said.

Kelly stood at his table, shuffled his notes and looked at Wereschuk.

"Mr. Wereschuk, I understand that you are a resident of Leila Street?"

"That's correct. I'm at 1584."

"1584. And in fact, your address is adjacent to the culvert where this accident occurred with Adam Young?"

"That's correct." he replied. Paul, at one time had worked for the Medical Examiner's office. An inquest was nothing new to him. His answers were straight to the point.

"And if I were to show you this photo in front of you here, if you can just take a look at that, is that area familiar to you?"

"That's correct. It's basically across the street."

"Okay. And are you familiar with this?"

"That's correct, I am."

"You're familiar with the culvert there? And is that the area that -- where the accident happened with Adam Young?"

"That's correct."

Kelly looked at Paul, " Sir, your name has surfaced in testimony today, indicating that at various times, you have had contact with certain City officials, I'll say, with respect to complaints you've had?

"Yes. We've spoken quite a few times." The court room was quiet.

"In fact, it's my understanding that, from the testimony earlier, that on April 21st, you had contacted the Mayor's office? Can you tell the Court exactly why you contacted the Mayor's office?"

Paul replied, "Basically, it essentially stemmed from concern over three things. Number one is we were flooding out in our area, and it happens persistently every year, since they put the school across there. Number two is we were concerned about our children in the area because of the constant flooding we had in the area, and that was our -- our major concerns again, you know, both you losing your basements and the fact that, you know, a child could get away, and we were scared that somebody was going to drown. That was our main concerns."

"With respect primarily to the second point that you raised, did you in fact raise that issue when you called the Mayor's office?"

"Unfortunately, in the heat of the moment, when we phoned and asked to speak to the Mayor, and they said that she was out of town, and at that point in time we said, "Well, we've gotten a hold of Councillors like Harry Lazarenko, Michael O'Shaughnessy, and we were getting nowhere, and what's it going to take, a death?" You know, like we were concerned about our children around the area. And it was like we wanted somebody to come down and correct all the problems, not just one or two of them. But like I say, out of the heat of the moment, we -- we did say we were concerned about residents, as we were talking. Like the neighbours right behind us and beside us, of course they all got young children, and we were talking the night before about this, and we were walking past the area, saying like, you know -- again, it was drowning more than anything, so ..."

Kelly asked, "I need to clarify an issue for myself. During your time -- around this time, April 21st, April 22nd, had you at any time seen kids playing within the culverts?"

"Not at the culvert itself, but in the area we saw children, like you know, they were school children and everything else. I mean children walk up and down the roads. There's always children around. You know, so -- I mean, it's a school, and that pretty well sums it up there. Children are there all the time. We've -- we've complained to the school, we've complained to the City."

"So during this time, you never actually saw kids playing in the culverts anywhere?

"No," Paul answered. "No, not in the culvert."

"In the particular culvert where this incident happened with Adam Young, were you aware of the culvert being -- running or --"

"No. We -- we were more concerned with -- in the picture, if you look over about -- I don't know what you'd say, maybe thirty feet, that culvert there, this --"

"Maybe if you could just point this out? Just turn it around so His Honour could see what you are pointing at."

Paul turned to the side, "This culvert that's right here, that's the one we're concerned about. It kept on plugging up, and they had -- the City continually had to come down and pull off the cover because there was all kinds of debris coming from the field and the construction just to Amber Trails. So what was happening is it would always keep plugging up with, you know, all kinds of debris and that. And what we were really concerned with was somebody was going to go down there, they were going to take off the -- move the debris, and they had it open several times, where it was wide open, you know, to let water go down it, and we were scared that if any of the children happened to accidentally slip, fall -- I mean, when you got a three year-old, they're not thinking, and if they get away from you .... That's what we were really terrified of. The last thing we ever suspected was that culvert, the little one."

"During the proceeding -- well, actually, I'll -- I'll say this, it's -- it's fair to say then, sir, that that area is bad for collection of water?" Kelly asked.

"Yes. We've been fighting over this for four years, but with deaf ears."

"And you've complained to the City on those aspects?"

"Continually. Almost every year."

"Have you, at any time, explicitly, sir, complained about children playing in the water to anybody?"

"We've -- we've -- said this several times. We've said like, you know -- again, our concern is like everybody knows what children are like. I mean no matter how -- how tight you are, but I mean there's a lot of times we see children who are not supervised, when they're walking around, throwing stones in, the kids are clowning around. And what happens is quite a few of the residents do take it upon themselves to yell at the kids, and get away from there."

Paul was getting emotional. His voice was becoming shaky and his head was lowering.

He continued, "But everybody kind of looks at you stupidly. Like when your child -- you're -- you know, you don't expect -- the obvious is the big culvert. The little one wasn't. It was basically a sleeping giant."

"The big one, you mean the one you have pointed out with the with the lid on it?"

"That's -- that's the one we were really concerned about, especially when they start pulling off the covers."

Judge Guy looked confused. He glanced at Wereschuk and asked, "But when they pulled off the cover, they were still there, were they not?"

Paul looked at Guy, "No. Sometimes they would leave. And that was why
we were so upset about these things.

Guy was shocked. He had to hear it again. "So they would take the top off and leave it off?"

"That's right. They would leave it off for a while and go away, and it was unsupervised," Paul answered.

Judge Guy kept looking at Paul, neither saying anything. The court room was quiet except for the whispers of two city lawyers. Guy looked at them, like a teacher stares down a group of annoying kids.

Kelly seemed to not know what to do next. After a few moments he continued. "Now, during those occasions, you would phone and advise the City of that?"

"Oh, yeah. It's not only me. Like all the neighbours phone, you know, from time-to-time and ..."

"Now, I understand you also had a discussion or a meeting with Councillor Lazarenko?"

"Yes. He was there on Sunday afternoon. As a matter of fact, we gave him the grand tour of residences, right from my house to the end of the block, that were flooding. We were showing him that -- the pressure that was created from out this area, the way the development is, and was flooding the streets and everything else, and so he came into our basements, looked at the flooding, said yes, this was nonsense and he was going to do something about it soon as he went down and saw the flooding at the Red River, and we -at that time, we had, you know, expect -- expressed our concern to him, there was about six or seven neighbours in the back, and we said to Harry then, you know, what's it going to take? You know, it's going to take a death to -- before somebody does something? I mean, this is four years of deaf ears, and -- and -- you're here now, Harry, like you can see the problem. And he gave us our assurance that everything would be taken care of, and unfortunately we haven't heard back from any of the Councillors since then."

Kelly paused and looked at the Judge's bench. "I have no more further questions, Your Honour. Thank you."

Judge Guy didn't even raise his head, " Mr. Guttman?!"

Dave stood up from his seat slowly, "Thank you, Your Honour. Mr. Wereschuk, just so we're not confused, the Red River flooding had nothing to do with what was going on, your street; is that correct?

Paul grinned, "No. I personally -- okay. If -- if you're talking personally, I believe, personally, it did have a lot to do with it, because everybody that -- in regard to City officials, were all out doing pressed moves and everything else. So to try to get a hold of somebody, even when we phoned the Mayor's office, we phoned her Monday morning, no reply. And we concerned -- we were concerned, and expressed that there was a problem, there was going to be an accident. It was -- we were concerned about our residents, our children, and she's down south, on a publicity tour of the flooding down south, when she should be concerned about our children in the taxpayers' area.

"I guess what I'm getting at, sir, is that the presence of the successive water on your particular street wasn't coming from the river, it was coming from the snow that was melting, this tremendous accumulation of snow?"

Paul answered, "Well, unfortunately, where the water is coming from is a man-made problem by the City of Winnipeg, and you would have to -- to look at the area to see that, but it -- it's a man-made problem."

"And it's a problem that you had experienced in previous years?"

"That's correct."

"So let's go back one year, to 1996. You had similar water levels; is that right?"

"No. Not true. Every year that they keep developing the area, it continually grows, and unfortunately, if you survey the area, we have no drainage on the south side. If you look at the north side, when they put in the school and built up the whole area, it created more flooding the first year. Then they popped in the development of Amber Trails, and what they do is they keep taking the mud from Amber Trails, moving it back into the field to block off the water coming in, so they can develop the new area, which forces the water around the school and back onto our place. Now they have put in the fire hall, which has increased it. With the massive snows, every year, we're getting worse problems than the year before."

"What I guess I'm getting at, sir, is having water in the ditches on the other side of the street is not a new problem, that's something that's taken place a number of times since the school has been present there; is that correct?"

"Since the school was there, yeah, it increases every year."

"Okay, sir. Now, in your view, ought there to be warning signs for these children that play in the area?" Dave asked.

"Yeah, you could put a warning sign up, but unfortunately, a three year-old can't read it."

"Fair enough. But school-aged children, presumably once they are past grade one or grade two can read?"

"Obviously, if -- I -- I guess it's -- as a resident, I'd have to say that was kind of naive, in the way of -- I don't know how to exactly explain it. I guess it's like drinking and driving. You know -- as a adult, you know not to drink and drive but I mean people still do."

"Sure."

"So even if a sign was there -- I mean when children are playing, they are not going to stop and read every sign that's -- that's posted."

Dave continued, "Okay. When you said earlier that complaints had been made to the City and the school, did you and your wife personally make any complaints to the school?"

"Yes, we did. Several occasions."

"And in addition to the City, as well?"

"That's correct," Paul answered.

"And to be fair, when Councillor Lazarenko came to see you on the Sunday, he was more concerned with the damage to your home and your neighbours' homes than what was going on across the street; is that fair?"

"No."

"That's not fair?"

"No."

"Please elaborate, sir," Dave asked.

"What happened is we explained to him that because of the snow build-up there, they did not clean our last block off of snow, and so like when the last snow storm hit, they left it plugged off, and it accumulated, and then we had to explain to Mr. Lazarenko that with all the water around, we were concerned with our children, as well. I mean like what -- what does the City have to do in order to -- I mean we can sit and talk about this all the time, but I mean our -- one of our major concerns was the fact that not only were we flooding out, but we have children, and we were concerned with our children, if anybody slips away. And so Mr. Lazarenko, at that time, did, the following day, get a grader in to open up the snow, and when he got that grader in to open up the snow and get the water to move, it just created a bigger problem, because now you opened it up from the backlash."

"As I understand it, you and the other residents on the block have not been able to resolve your problems with the City; is that fair?"

"No. Nobody will talk to us. They will not give us any

information. They -- they talked to us up to the time that this tragedy happened, and now they -- they -- they won't even give us the time of day."

"And have you now engaged counsel and commenced your own claim against the City?"

"Yes, we did. We haven't sued. We did get counsel, and we took our video tapes and everything to them."

Dave paused then looked at Paul, "Is there anything, in your view, that the City could have done to avert this particular tragedy, sir?"

"Yes, several. Number one is the City is allowing zoning and development without increasing the proper sewage systems. They've known about this for years. The City also knows the ongoing battle they've had with the residents, to try to get the residents to pay for new streets and sidewalks because of the new development expansion, that the City is ignoring. They're trying to get each individual person to pay for it. And that's basically why some of this stuff is happening. As well, the City is allowing development in the area without proper drainage, without proper protection, and they are more worried about expanding those areas than they are about the continuing existing problems, and when we try to speak to them about it, and tell them, and express the concerns, when we go to the school board and mention it to them, we're kind of ignored in the point that, well, sour grapes, you're flooded out, and that's it, fine. And to me, they've got to -- they've got to teach what they preach, and they don't."

"Sir, if you want to take a look at that picture just for a moment." Dave handed Paul the picture of the culvert on Roblin and Harstone Road that I had taken. "Do you know of any -- I'll use the term culvert. You can see the pipe there."

"Um-hum," Paul said as he looked at the picture.

"Pipes in your area that have grates over them?"

"No. no, I don't. This one has one now."

"I understand it has one now," Dave stated.

"Um-hum."

"Do you know if any other ones do?"

"No, I don't."

"And I take it your area is replete with small children? There's a number of young families in that area?"

"Oh, it's full of them. Full of them," Paul answered as he continued to look at the picture.

"Thank you," Dave said as he sat down. "Those are all the questions I have, sir."

Judge Guy turned to Marvin and his colleague, Carswell. "Mr. Samphir?"

"I have a few questions. May I have just a minute?"

Marvin started conferring with Kim Carswell. He was pointing out the notes he had made. The grin was back.

"Mr. Wereschuk, you have indicated you have called the City or complained to someone at the City on several occasions in around the time of -- of the incident, April 22nd?" He wasn't looking at Paul. He was smiling at his notes.

"That's correct," Paul stated.

"Firstly, when you say you contacted someone in the Mayor's office on April 21, '97, did you get the name of the person you spoke to?"

"No. Normally you ask to speak to the Mayor."

"So you didn't get the name of the person?"

"No, I didn't. It was the same girl who was answering the phones Tuesday morning, though, as well."

"So it was a woman you spoke to in the Mayor's office?"

"That's correct. And somehow I have the impression it was the secretary -- or not the secretary, the -- like a girl answering the phones while everybody was out."

Marvin looked at his notes and smiled. He held up a sheet of paper with a few type written lines at the top. He held it up, and waved it as he said, "However, you did call to -- call to the City on other occasions, and I have a copy of a -- at least a conversation that you had with a Mr. Ed Deneschuk; do you remember that, on April 19th, 1997, when you called to complain about possible flooding at your home?"

"Not necessarily, but --"

Marvin wasn't going to let him finish his answer. He interrupted with his own answer, "But you -- you were being flooded, or you were being flooded or you were concerned about flooding at that time?"

"Well, we were phoning from -- actually, sir, we were phoning everybody and anybody from Saturday night, at nine o'clock at night, right through until Tuesday morning."

"I see, " Marvin grinned.

"So it's possible I spoke to him. I mean, we spoke -- we phoned Sewer, Waterworks. We phoned Harry Lazarenko. We phoned Michael O'Shaughnessy. We phoned -- I mean if there was a City official I could get a hold of, I phoned him."

"This call was made, at least according to the record I have, approximately April 19th, 1997, at 2240, which would be ten forty in the evening."

"Okay. That's possible, yeah."

Marvin stated, "And I'm going to suggest to you that at no time did you raise any concern about problems with children drowning, et cetera. Your -- your only concern at the time was the fact that the water was coming in and the sewers were plugged?"

"No, I -- I agree with that, because that was 10:30 at night. We were all flooding out." Paul was getting angry.

Marvin continued to grin. He was getting to Paul. "I see. And I then have a second note of a telephone discussion that you had with someone on April 21st, 1997, at 8:52 in the morning, and this is with Ann Gulenchyn, at -- and indicates that again you were call -- calling about sewer backup problems, wanting to know what's being done, have someone come out, to call them, and that was at the Board of Commissioners' office, and no mention made, I understand, at all, that any concerns about problems with children in the area?"

From where I was sitting I could see the piece of paper Marvin had pulled out. It was blank. Nothing was on this note. He waved it around the court, careful not to show it. He was playing a bluff.

"Well, no. At that particular time, what we did was we were concerned about the present. We were flooding out. But I mean every time you make a phone call, you don't phone and say, Somebody is going to drown, right away," Paul answered. I had no way of letting him know what Samphir was doing.

Marvin continued, "But yet you -- I just want to make sure I understand you. But yet, you say on April 21st, the same day that you call -- contacted the Board of Commissioners, through Ann Gulenchyn, and you say you told the Mayor's office you were afraid that someone was going to drown, you didn't mention the same thing to the Board of Commissioners' office?"

"Oh, well, you know, like I didn't have it rehearsed, if that's what you're asking me."

"I see, Marvin stated. He laughed, "I'm not suggesting you had it rehearsed because --"

"No." Paul shook his head. "No. It's -- it's just I -- I think the situation of what you're saying here right now is when you're flooding out, you're phoning Works and Operations, and you're saying you have a concern with flooding, because that was what was happening at the time. We had no power, no water and we wanted somebody down there. But if you're saying when Harry Lazarenko was there, and we had five other family -- you know, different families around, when we stated that concern, do you have that there, by any chance?" Paul was almost yelling. Samphir had gotten to him.

Marvin grinned, "He was there on the 20th."

"It was a Sunday. Do you have that record there, too, or when we --"

Again Marvin wasn't about to let him finish, "No, I don't have records from Mr. Lazarenko's office."

Paul answered, "Well, that was one of the problems we had. We requested all the records, too, as well, from the City, for all this, and all of a sudden, nobody had them for us. And that's what we had requested from the City, right from the Board of Commissioners, up," Paul was on the edge. "But the fact of the matter still remains, we did speak to Harry Lazarenko on that Sunday, and we did have all kinds of community family -- like different people around who did all concern ourselves about this problem. So it wasn't just flooding. Flooding was our main concern at the time, and -- and we said it at the time, too. You know, at the heat of the moment, we said things Monday that we regretted saying now because unfortunately something did happen. We never wanted it to happen, but it did, and we still believe that there can be a worse tragedy this coming year if we get more snow or water."

"You -- when you said you made complaints to the school, were they the same complaints that you suggested you made to the City about the --"

"Yeah. Actually, the -- the school, we've had problems with the children for a while now, so we've had everything from people writing on signs to kids -- children cutting through yards to -- you know, some of the bigger kids roughing up. You know, just everyday children things. But they were all concerns that we had stressed to the school, saying that, you know, like we would like to see a little tighter rein put on the children, to the fact that, you know, they're damaging all our area and everything else, and that was a concern to the neighbourhood, as well, is like they -- they would go behind garages and everything else, and we were asking that the school at least say, like you know, quit cutting through neighbours' yards or stuff like that. And unfortunately we -- we got nowhere. In other words, the school said, like, you know, what's on school time is school time, what is not school time is not school time."

Marvin grinned, "Mr. Wereschuk, do you have anything in writing where you set out your complaints in around the time of April 21st, 1997, either to the school division or the City, by setting out your complaints, where you list all the concerns you had with the flooding and/or other issues in the area?" Samphir knew. He knew the residents had applied through the Access to Information Act for all the documents relating to this incident. He also knew that this request was denied, just like my request was. He knew. He was the one who denied the requests. This only made the smile bigger.

"No. What we did do is we did a journal from the time the flooding started right up until the time the flood was over, right until that Tuesday afternoon, and it was due to the fact that the City has continually done this to us. It's the same old story of they have something in writing or they have something on record but we never do, so now the whole neighbourhood, everybody concerned all started making journals.

Paul continued, "That's why we did the videotaping, as well, of the area, and the flooding, and the snow removal and who was there at the time, for this reason. It was -- we have found -- we have been stonewalled from the City for several years, so now we decided, instead of being stonewalled, we were going to do the same thing they did. Instead of saying Harry Lazarenko said this, having a picture of Harry Lazarenko there was worth a million words, with more than one witness around as to what was said was worth more than a million words. It was the same thing the City does to us," Paul said.

He continued, "They seem to always have a record of something when it benefits them, but if you request it, they won't release it to us, and that was one of the problems we really had."

"Those are my questions," Marvin sat, smiling.

Kelly stood and faced Judge Guy, "That's the extent of the witnesses the Crown has subpoenaed for today, Your Honour."

Judge Guy checked the clock, then said, " Okay. Adjourned 'til ten o'clock tomorrow morning." He stood and left the court room.

As the gallery was exiting the court, Dave turned to me, "Let's go talk."

I turned to Michelle. She had a look of disgust on her face. She was staring at Samphir. He was laughing about something as he packed his notes up. Michelle headed straight for him.

"You disgust me!" She was now standing in front of the table where Marvin was. "You think the death of a child is funny? You've been laughing all day. Maybe you should wipe that stupid grin off your face and start taking this matter seriously," she yelled.

Marvin was speechless. He packed his notes and exited the court room as fast as he could.

Kelly was still in the room, and had stood silently as the confrontation was going on.

He looked at me and said, "That was very appropriate."

"He deserved that," the court clerk said.

17

"Good morning," Judge Guy said as he entered the court room Dave stood, "Good morning, Your Honour."

"Good morning, Your Honour," Moar said. "Your Honour, today I'll just indicate so Your Honour is aware. It's anticipated today, Your Honour, that witnesses that will be called, will be Councillors Lazarenko and O'Shaughnessy, and then subsequent to that, Your Honour, will be Tom Pearson, who is head of the City Water Works and Operations who will be bringing a series of charts to explain the situation and, finally, Your Honour, I anticipate Bill Carroll will be called today. I am hoping that depending on the time, we'll finish today. If Your Honour will call Councillor Lazarenko."

Before the court room had been opened, I had spoken to Mike and Harry in the hall.

"I don't know why we have to go through this," Harry said. "They know they're at fault. I'll never understand why they don't just admit it and fix them. This is stupid."

"Marvin's worried. He knows we're going to have to pay. It's just a matter of how much," Mike said.

I replied, "Now you know what it's been like. I've had to fight this and they just ignore the situation. All I want is to have these things fixed. Why won't they do it".

"It's just the way they do things," Harry said. "I don't even know why I have to be here."

The court clerk addressed Harry as he entered the court room. "Please stand in the witness box. Take the Bible in your right hand and state your name to the Court."

"Harry Lazarenko."

"Mr. Lazarenko," Kelly started. "I understand you've been a City councillor for some twenty-odd years; would that be correct?"

Harry confirmed.

Kelly continued, "And I understand that your ward or jurisdiction is not the area where the event occurred with respect to Adam Young?"

"Correct."

"I also understand that you are head of the Works and Operations Committee -- or a member."

"Correct."

"Okay. It's my understanding, Sir, yesterday we had an individual testifying by the name of Mr. Paul Wereschuk indicating an incident where you attended to his residence approximately April 20th to deal with a complaint?"

"Yes, and that was on a Sunday morning."

"Would you tell the Court exactly how you were notified of this complaint and what you did."

Harry replied, "I received a call at one o'clock Sunday morning and -- with the complainant telling me that their basements were getting flooded. He said he was not able to get hold of his area councillor because as he was out of town. So I took the complaint and I notified our emergency crew to take that into account to see what they could do and then I called him back and I told him what I had done. At 9:00 am. that same day, Sunday morning, I received a call from the same individual saying that nothing was done, the water was still coming up in the basement, and he begged me to come and take a look. And so later on, sometime before noon, I did go there with my brother-in-law. I took a drive through there and I went down the back lane and I met three individual people that I went into their houses. I saw the water in the basement and I had said that I'll phone the department again to see if they can rectify the problem."

"Okay. Did you do that, Sir?"

"Yes, I did."

"One of the issues that arose yesterday, Sir, was that, according to Mr. Wereschuk's evidence, he indicated to the Court that, in fact, he did call you and complained about water in the basement but also raised the issue of safety of children and asked you to address that issue."

"I don't recall that, Sir, at all."

"You don't recall Mr. Wereschuk raising that issue with you?"

"No, not whatsoever. I was there just strictly the basement flooding and I was in the back lane. I didn't go in other -- no other area."

Kelly asked, "So at no time were you in the front of Leila Avenue?"

"I just drove through there, Sir. I drove through there to get into the back lane of their residence and that was all. I didn't stop by. I didn't walk around there, nothing.

"When you went by that day, did you happen to notice opposite where Mr. Wereschuk was living, the level of water?"

"Yes, I did see there was water out in the field and in the ditches."

"Okay. Are you able to comment on how high the water was in the ditches?"

"Well, I would say that the water was pretty well level -- close to being to the level of the road. The ditches, mind you, are not that big in there, you know. I've got that
in my ward, too, you know, where they -- where there's ditches where the water fills at that time of the year."

"Now, briefly, Sir, if, in fact, such a complaint was raised with you with respect to safety to children with respect to the opposite side of the road, the culvert area, what, if anything, would you have done or could you have done on that date?"

"The only thing I would have been able to do is to refer this to the department that do take complaints and to say that there is -- might be an immediate danger, try to get it rectified immediately."

"Okay. And this would be -- to my understanding you have an emergency department, is that right?" Kelly asked.

Harry answered, "Yes, we do."

"And that's accessible 24 hours a day?"

"24 hours a day, correct."

"Have you used them in the past?"

"Oh, I -- very often."

"And how quickly have they responded?" Kelly asked

"To my knowledge," Harry replied, "they have responded as soon as they can because -- it depends on what time of the year. Like at this time, they had maybe hundreds of other calls. This one I guess they didn't respond immediately because otherwise I would not have received a call from this individual person at nine o'clock that very same day."

"Okay. And again, just from your recollection, you don't recall any issue of safety of children being raised?"

"No, none whatsoever."

"And it's my understanding this is the only contact you've had with Mr. Wereschuk?" Kelly asked.

"Yes, I never met the gentleman. I just met him there that very same day. He did call my office that following Monday and he had stated in the voice mail - my assistant handled that call, tried to call him back a few times - stating that they were batting zero, that there was nothing that has been rectified, please help us. We need help and that was the end of it. Because then after that the councillor for the area had taken it over when he come back -- come back into the city that Sunday night or Monday morning."

"Okay. Thank you, Sir," Kelly finished.

"Mr. Guttman," Judge Guy stated.

"Thank you, Your Honour," Dave replied as he stood to address Lazarenko.

"Councillor, you've indicated you spent twenty plus years with the city council. Have you had occasion to deal with numerous complaints from constituents and residents over that time?

"Oh, yes, many. Many complaints."

Dave asked, "Can you tell us a little about the procedure that takes place when you receive a complaint. What exactly do you do in addition to perhaps making a telephone call at that point in time?"

"Well, what our responsibility is, we address the concern that is raised to us. What I do is I pass it on to the proper department for immediate action."

"Does the department report back to you?"

"If we're asked to have that reporting, yes, they do."

"Okay. Did you ask that the emergency department report back to you in this particular case?"

"No, I didn't because it was not my ward. I just relayed the message. In this case, Sir, I was a messenger, that I was helping out a colleague of mine and I took the complaint, the complaint that the residents had, and he had taken that over, and it would have been up to him to get that report."

"Obviously, this was a great tragedy, Councillor. A young boy perished. What, as a member of the Works and Operations Committee, are you aware of in terms of Works and Operations attempting to remedy this situation in the ensuing months after the tragedy?"

Harry paused. He had to think of what to say. He had to be careful. "My understanding is that we've -- we did have a meeting and it was raised to us that the -- that they were going to correct the problems. The Commissioner had indicated to us that a consultant was hired to take a look at the -- and report back to the administration to see the number of culverts that may be in the same -- same condition, and they were to remedy and try to fix as many as they can immediately before freeze-up."

"And is it fair to say, Councillor, that, to your knowledge, no consultant was hired until after this inquest was called?"

"I believe that is correct."

Dave stated, "Is it fair to say, Councillor, that at one point you were told to watch your comments in regards to this matter because of the potential for a lawsuit or legal liability?"

"It was mentioned at the Committee level that this may land up in court and be careful what you say and -- but we were not directed to keep our mouths shut or anything to that -- for that matter. We were just told the consequences we might be faced with that -- if we speak out of turn."

Finally! Everything that I had been saying was now out. Public record. A sense of relief over whelmed me and I started to cry. Michelle reached for my hand. Marvin glanced over and grinned.

"Can you tell me if you're aware, Sir, if any of these culverts have been covered with grating or grills or anything of that nature?"

Harry replied, "No. I had spoken to -- I had spoken to administration. I had said that if they would take a look any place where it's open, can you rectify them, and they said they would be reporting back to the Committee."

"But you yourself have received no report in that regard of any of these pipes being capped, if you want to use that term?"

"No. No, none whatsoever."

"Does that concern you, Sir?"

"Well, yes, everything concerns me as far as, you know, dealing with safety. You know in this case -- in this case there is a concern because a life has -- a life has been lost, so whatever has to be done should be rectified immediately, as soon as possible."

"In fact, Sir, the area in question has been subject to flooding for a number of years. That's what you were told by the residents; is that correct?" Dave asked.

"Yes. I was told that the spring run-off that they get, you know, there was a continuous problem at that time of the year."

"And were you also told by the residents that they have continued to complain year after year and are less than satisfied with the action taken by city hall in that regard?"

"Well, this individual person that called me, he had indicated -- he said that he's been complaining yearly of the problem and he was told that it was going to be rectified once they complete the work in that area."

"And as a councillor, Sir, all you can do is lobby on behalf of your constituents and ask questions and try and push forward but, in fact, any measures to correct dangerous situations are well outside your province; is that fair?"

"That's correct," Harry stated quietly.

"Thank you. Those are my questions," Dave stated to Judge Guy

Judge Guy motioned to Harry, "Thank you, Sir. Any questions, Mr. Samphir?"

Marvin replied, "We have no questions."

Judge Guy stared at Samphir for a few moments. Kelly stood to address the bench.

"I'll call the next witness in, Your Honour."

"Step into the witness box and take the Bible in your right hand. State your name for the Court," the clerk asked.

"Mike O'Shaughnessy."

Kelly stood to face Mike in the witness box. "Mr. O'Shaughnessy, again I understand that you've actually been a councillor within the City for, in total, some twenty odd years, twenty-four years?"

"Eighteen years over the last twenty-four."

"Eighteen over the last twenty-four. And, in fact, you're the councillor for the ward where the tragic incident involving Adam Young occurred?"

"Yes."

"And that you were in such capacity on April 22nd of 1997?"

"Yes, I was."

Kelly continued, "Sir, I just want to discuss prior to April 22nd, 1997. There's been some issues raised through prior witnesses that area -- citizens living within that area have had contact with yourself with respect to complaints of not only flooding within that area but potential danger for children in that area."

Mike replied, "I have no recollection of the latter of anything about potential danger, but there were calls about basement flooding in the homes on Leila Avenue."

"And how long has that issue been a live issue?"

"To the best of my recollection this year was the first time that there was -- that there were complaints about the basement flooding."

"So for example in 1996, you don't recall receiving any complaints from individuals such as a Mr. Wereschuk or any of the residents on 1500 Leila, of a flooding?"

"Not specifically, no."

What was he saying? Mike knew there had been complaints for years about the excess water. In 93 he sent me out to calm certain residents that had been complaining.

"Do you recall at any point, Sir, that the issue of the safety of children being raised with the culverts being full of water?" Kelly asked.

"No," Mike stated.

"Never?"

"Never."

Kelly knew Mike wasn't tell the truth. *I had mentioned the complaints to him in a previous meeting we had before the inquest.*

He continued to question Mike. "Okay. Just for clarification purposes, and maybe I should have done this earlier. You -- my understanding is you know Mr. Young?"

"Yes, I do," Mike answered.

"And, in fact, you know him on a personal level?"

"On a personal level. He paused. I'm sure he didn't know how far to go with his answer. "He, his family, and he did work for me at City Hall."

"Okay. And in what capacity did he work for you?"

"My executive assistant."

"And when did that relationship cease, the business relationship?"

"When was the last provincial election? A few months before the provincial election. I believe that was in '93, was it?"

"Now, subsequent to this -- to the incident with respect to Adam Young, has your office or yourself had any discussions with a Mr. Benedet?" Kelly asked

Mike was surprised. "I do not recall. He had to think. "I've been told that he sent a letter and that I replied to it but that would not be unusual. My office receives anywhere from forty to a hundred phone calls a day and letters on a regular basis."

"When you say that you may have received a letter and replied, what do you mean by that? Like I guess it's a little unusual that you wouldn't recall. My understanding is you have an assistant."

"Yes."

"And is it safe to say that your assistant actually handles most of your correspondence?"

"Handles all of the incoming phone calls and would open my mail and see letters before I would but certainly would not reply under my name. If there is a reply under my name, I would have written or approved. In most cases, written it myself."

"So there's no way that would ever occur. That a letter would go out under your name without you knowing it, that you're aware of, anyway?"

"Better not," Mike grinned as he replied to Kelly's question.

"The information that I've received with respect to Mr. Benedet is he corresponded with your office with respect to a design to cover the culverts, to cap them, for lack of a better word."

"I did receive -- I didn't recall the name, but I did receive a proposal to cap culverts."

"Yeah."

"I believe that was after the incident."

"Yeah."

"Yes."

"My understanding is that this was around May the 9th or so."

"Yes, and that was forwarded -- I didn't -- sorry, I didn't recall the name, but, yes, I did receive that. It was forwarded to the Water and Waste Department and it was -- and I did reply to that correspondence, yes."

"Is it the practice within your office, Sir, that your assistants may have received calls and briefly discussed it with you and then take action?"

"Or just take action directly. There's a number of phone calls. They fall into, if I may, into three categories and that would be: people expressing an opinion on something in which case if it's direct, they jot down the opinion and it's just handed over for my information. I look at it, and depending on what the issue -- this happens a lot. The other thing is direct complaints such as snow clearing, sewer back-up, et cetera, where my assistant would immediately phone the department themselves or the call centre depending on what it is. And those involving policy or involving where the constituent was not satisfied with how a department handled it, those would go on to me."

"With respect to if you received calls that required immediate action, those would be the ones that would be forwarded to the appropriate call centres? " Kelly asked.

"Yes, as long as it was a standard complaint. If it didn't involve a request for a change in City policy it would go right to the department."

"And that would be the extent of your action with respect to that, it would be forwarding it on?"

"Unless I hear back from the constituent saying that they are not satisfied with the action taken and then I get personally involved at that point."

"With respect to that, your fellow councillor testified earlier, when you send in a complaint, do you ever request back -- or feedback on the result of it or is it --"

"Sometimes. It does happen. I will -- if I'm passing it on directly, I will ask that the department let me know when it's done, if it's a repeat complaint, especially."

Kelly's questioning continued for a few more moments. He was trying to get a handle on how incoming complaints were handled.

Finally Kelly just asked, "Is it possible, Sir, that a complaint could come into your office and you not be aware of it?"

Mike replied, "Yes. I spend most of my day in meetings."

Kelly thanked Mike and sat down.

It was Dave's turn. He stood and turned to the witness box. "Councillor, do you recall attending a meeting with Tom Pearson in the company of Rob Young a day or two after the tragedy occurred?"

"Yes."

"And is it fair to say that you took the step of arranging that meeting for Rob in an effort to find out what had happened and what could be done to prevent things like this from happening in the future?" Dave was getting right to the point, fast.

"Yes. I did it to alleviate Rob's -- some of Rob's anxiety and give him some purpose. We are friends as well as..."

Dave interrupted, "And at that point during that meeting, is it fair to say that you told Tom Pearson that they better take a hard look at this site and other similar sites and as quickly as possible because the spring run-off wasn't finished?

"Yes, I believe it was, Forget the reports. Just get it done."

"And I take it on behalf of your own constituent area and on behalf of the Young family, you've continued to ask questions about what's being done about this situation over the past five months; is that fair?"

"Yes, I have."

"And what responses had you received prior to the end of the summer?"

"That an engineering study was being done; that the-- there would not be a possibility of a similar occurrence until next spring, and that the actions would be taken before freeze-up this year."

"Okay. At any point in time were you told by anyone not to comment on this matter in a public forum because of potential legal liability?"

"No." Mike paused before continuing. "But that would go without saying."

"Now, as I understand it, one of your many duties you're involved in and you're actually chairman of the committee that deals with the police department; is that correct?"

"Yes."

"Can you give us any reason or any understanding as to why my friend, Crown counsel, received only half of the police report in regard to this matter until a further request was made?"

"I heard about that." Mike was getting uncomfortable. "I made an -- I E-mailed the chief of police and the commissioner on the matter and received a reply that it was a clerical error, that the files were kept in two different areas and that one file was forwarded and the other wasn't, and that upon the request that -- because of that, the entire file would be forwarded."

"Do you believe it's a coincidence, Sir, that the part that wasn't forwarded dealt with all that had been done by City employees at the site before and after the incident in question?"

"I don't know the report. I hadn't seen either part of it, so that would be - having watched Perry Mason - speculation on my part."

"Fair enough, Sir. I thought I heard you say when my friend was asking you questions that you didn't recall any previous complaints about flooding prior to 1997.

"I don't recall, from this specific block, complaints about flooding that would be
hazardous to children."

"But, in fact, there had been numerous complaints over the years from residents about basement flooding and problems with water run-off in that particular area; is that fair?"

"In the general area. This and the -- there's about five blocks to Leila and it has come from all of those areas over time, yes."

"Yes. And, in fact, when Mr. Young worked for you approximately four years ago, there were one or more occasions where you actually sent him to see some of these residents and examine some of the flood damage?"

"I don't know about flood damage but I do know that he was sent out by me and both also went out on his own initiative on a number of complaints."

"Have you yourself been contacted by Works and Operations and shown any remedial measures that have been made in your ward?"

"No," Mike said quietly. There was a meeting of Works and Operations just recently where City officials appeared. Mr. Pearson, who I believe will be here later, appeared and showed what -- well, didn't show but explained what works were being done and would be done and I did attend that meeting."

"But to your knowledge you have not seen any physical evidence of any remedial measures; is that fair, in your ward?"

"The only measures I've seen are the -- the picture of the culvert with two long spikes driven through it which I'm -- have been told were Mr. Young's work."

"I believe what you just referred to, Councillor, is Exhibit 9 which is a photograph taken shortly after the water had --I'm also showing you Exhibit 10 and this depicts a similar pipe at Harstone Road and Roblin in Charleswood and you can see it's covered with a grate. Have you ever been given any explanation by anyone in Works and Operations as to why the pipe in question located where Adam Young passed away wasn't capped in a similar manner?"

"No, I was told that we had 176 similar situations in the City and that none of them were capped.

"None of them?" Dave asked.

"So I'm surprised to see this."

"Are you satisfied, Councillor O'Shaughnessy, that everything that can be done is being done to prevent this from happening in the future?"

Mike paused before committing to his answer. "I'm satisfied that I've been told that it is being done, but I will follow up on that to see the physical evidence once I'm told that it's been completed."

"In fact," Dave stated, "you're reserving judgement based on your lengthy experience on City council in terms of things actually getting done as opposed to being told they will be done; is that fair?

"No." Mike stopped. He dropped his head. "But it's true."

"Is it your opinion, Sir, that these remedial measures would have been taken or undertaken or proposed to be undertaken, had this inquest not been called?"

"Yes, they would have."

FOR MY SON

"And you base that on?" Dave asked.

"The fact that," he stopped and turned to look at me. I saw the tears. Mike started to cry. "- the fact of who it happened to and that I would have made sure it happened."

Dave stopped to give him time. "Thank you very much, Sir. Those are my questions."

Any questions, Mr. Samphir?" Judge Guy asked.

"No!"

The court room was silent.

Judge Guy turned to Kelly. "Call your next witness Mr. Moar."

"Just step into the witness box, remain standing, take the Bible in your right hand and state your name to the Court."

"Devi Sharma."

Kelly started. "Ms. Sharma, I understand that you are the assistant to Councillor O'Shaughnessy?"

"Yes, I am."

"And how long have you acted in that capacity?"

"I've worked for Councillor O'Shaughnessy since April of 1995 on a full time basis," Devi replied.

"Okay. So is it safe to say that you are well aware of his ward and the areas that he covers?"

"Yes, very much so."

"Now, Councillor O'Shaughnessy testified earlier that one of your responsibilities is taking most of the incoming calls and, in essence, screening them and directing them to the appropriate departments. So that would be a fair comment to make?"

"Yes, that's correct."

"And, in fact, one of the type of calls Councillor O'Shaughnessy talked about was calls that require immediate attention to areas."

"Yes."

Devi was obviously nervous. We spoke prior to the hearing. She didn't know why they had wanted her here and I tried to calm her by telling her to just tell the truth. I don't think that helped.

"With respect to those calls, Ma'am, do you, at any point, undertake actions on your own with respect to those?"

"Yes, I do."

"Okay You're aware of the incident that occurred April 22nd on Leila, in fact, the photo depicts the area?"

"Yes."

"That was the death of Adam Young. Prior to that incident, Ma'am, do you recall receiving any complaints or concerns from area residents concerned with safety of the children in -- the ditches being filled with water?"

"No, we didn't receive any calls."

Kelly looked stunned. Three people had already testified to receiving calls of complaint. Mike confirmed the complaints. He testified that his assistant received them.

What is she doing?

"Okay. Now, let me ask you, prior to this incident, do you recall receiving complaints from area residents dealing with flooding, high water levels, in the area of Leila?"

"No, I don't."

"You don't recall ever?"

"At some time -- that happened some time ago and I deal with over 50 calls a day. I don't recall," she said.

The day Adam died I stood three feet away from Devi, in Mike's office, and heard her on the phone with a resident, discuss the water. How could she forget?

Kelly continued, "So no call sticks out in your mind with respect to that?"

"Not that I remember."

"Do you recall ever receiving a phone call from a Paul Wereschuk? Does that name ring a bell to you?"

"No, it doesn't."

"During your time with Councillor O'Shaughnessy, do you ever recall receiving phone calls dealing with manhole covers being left open and unattended?"

"No," Devi looked like she was ready to cry.

"Nothing like that. Okay. When you receive calls that initially come in, is there a form that you fill out with respect to those type of..."

"We tried keeping a log sometime ago but it just -- it wasn't working, there was just a massive paper trail. So I take the calls down and I deal with them immediately and we don't record them after that unless it's something that needs further follow-up."

"So those type of things you would actually write down and keep some sort of log on?"

"Right."

"Okay. I have a copy of a form here and I believe my friend has the original. Can I have you just take a look at this. Is this familiar to you, at all?" Kelly handed a small sheet of paper, called an Action Inquiry. This inquiry is used to record calls that come into a Councillor's office. This particular inquiry had been written up by Devi handwritten

Devi's eyes opened wide. "This is not my handwriting."

"It's not?"

"This is a type of action inquiry I would fill out. We had someone else working in the office at the time, Darlene Waters. This is her handwriting."

I left the court room. I didn't want to hear anymore. I couldn't.

18

"Mr. Pearson, I understand that you are the manager of the Water and Sewer Division here in the City of Winnipeg?"
"That's correct."

Kelly called Pearson to the stand shortly after 11:00 o'clock in the morning. I had ridden in the elevator with Samphir and Pearson first thing that morning. Samphir had been strutting Pearson and his charts around the Law Courts building since 9:00. I have a feeling Samphir expected Pearson to be his saviour, the one who would explain to the judge and the public what a wonderful job this organization had done. Normally a smile like Marvin's would light up a room.

Not this room, though.

Kelly stood beside Pearson in the witness box, "Can you explain to His Honour what exactly your job entails, Sir."

Pearson replied, "I'm responsible for the operation and the maintenance and the upgrading of the water distribution system, the waste water collection system and the pipe land drainage system for the City."

"Now, you and I, of course, have spoken on one previous

occasion?"

"Yes."

"In fact, I met with you down at the City law offices; is that right?"

"That's correct."

The city law office? I think Kelly through that in for Dave and I.

"And we discussed much of the incident with respect to Adam Young and the City systems?"

"Yes, we did."

"And I understand you brought a series of charts today."

"Yes."

"Perhaps you can begin by using your charts here, Sir, and explaining to His Honour where this incident occurred. I understand that you have a chart there and you can feel free to go over there, Sir."

It took a few moments for Pearson to set up his charts and get organized.

Pearson stood in front of his charts. He was not seated in the witness box like the other witnesses had been. It seemed like he was going to give a lecture rather than testify. This must have been the way they rehearsed it.

Pearson started, "I believe that the photo of the site has already been distributed and at the forefront of that photo is the fire station and behind it is a school."

"In this particular drawing, the fire station is located here; the school is here. Leila Avenue runs across the bottom of the drawing and the Allan Blye Drive runs up this side, so north is this way."

"What you see here is -- depicts our interpretation from pictures of the extent of the water that existed on the day of the accident on April 22nd. And the light shading, as you see here, is at a different depth than these dark pockets along here. The light shading is about a foot deep, give or take, and the dark pockets that you see here and here are about waist deep, say roughly a metre in depth."

"And by way of explanation, the reason for that is that this ditch which runs along Leila is really a shallow swale except at the points where it drains, and to the -- right in the vicinity of the culvert where the accident occurred, there is a depression that was created when that culvert was installed and that's where you see approximately a 20 foot length of deeper water, if you will, and on this side, again, there's a deeper stretch adjoining a manhole with a catch basin which drains this ditch. So that's what we see there. We -- in order to under --"

Judge Guy interrupted, "Before you go on, that manhole that you're talking about now, where is that located? Is that on the road?"

"This one?" Pearson asked.

"Yes."

"That's in the ditch."

"In the ditch."

"Yeah. And there's a catch basin which leads up to that manhole and it drains --"

Judge Guy again interrupted, "For example, if you can look in that photograph, please, and about the fourth picture on, can you see that manhole in the ditch? Is that the manhole that we're talking about?"

Pearson responded, "Yes, it is."

"Okay. Thank you," Judge Guy said.

Pearson continued, "In considering, I guess, how we were going to respond to this incident in terms of mitigative action, we believed that it was fairly important to understand what happened that day and, accordingly, we reviewed many reports. And our interpretation of what happened, and that's all this is, is that there were three fellows that entered the water to the west of the culvert. They progressed eastward. They noticed some styrofoam in the deep area, probably entrained in a whirlpool, which we estimate to be about a 6 inch diameter whirlpool from the information that we received. As they progressed to the west, they encountered the deeper water. Two of the fellows, I believe, headed back the other way."

Pearson paused then looked at his chart. "Adam Young was caught up in a strong current at this location, and when they endeavoured to save him from the current which was drawing him towards the culvert our impression is that Adam Young was reaching out to these two fellows and, accordingly, had his arms extended at the time and subsequently was drawn into the culvert with his arms extended in that fashion."

"That's, I think, an important issue relative to explaining the dimensions of the culvert, vis-a-vis the incident. Most of our -- and that culvert is a 16 inch culvert and, you know, 16 inches on most people, myself included, is about here in terms of an overall dimension." Was he using the fact that Adam's arms were extended as the reason?

Pearson continued, "In fact I have a tape measure. If you like I can illustrate that; it doesn't matter."

Judge Guy responded with a puzzled look, "No."

Pearson stopped. Judge Guy's response seemed to throw him off.

"In any event, most people wouldn't fit into a 16 inch culvert with our arms down. Of course with your arms extended you become a narrower individual, in essence, and that certainly would allow him to fit down the 16 inch culvert without any difficulty. We'll speak a little more about the hydraulics later, but the flow in the vicinity of that culvert, based on the information that has been developed by our consultant, appears to have been quite high, in the order of 4 metres per second right at the culvert inlet. And that's, I guess, for illustration purposes, you know, you would cross a 12 foot room in one second if you were caught up in that current, so it's quite high." There was several gasps from the gallery. Not many people knew how powerful the force was.

Pearson went on, "It translates to a significant what we call drag-forces on an individual. The current acts across the front of you, in essence, or the side of you, depending on how you're facing. We estimate that the -- that those drag-forces were in the order of - and these are soft numbers because of the science - but we estimate that those forces were between one and two hundred pounds acting on Adam at the time, depending on how close he was to the culvert. So there would have been some strong forces acting on him, and given his position holding onto another fellow, certainly he would have been carried with the current into the culvert. So that's -- that's, in terms of background, what we think happened."

The actual numbers shocked the court room. 12 foot room in one second, 200 pounds of pressure! Everyone was shocked.

Including the Judge.

Judge Guy sat up, "Can I just interrupt for a second --"

Pearson responded, "Yeah."

"We had a young man here, the second witness, he was a very small young man, so I guess the Court -- from the point of 16 inches the young man that was here would have went through that in a shot because he was quite small in stature and so I understand your point, but -"

"Yeah, I'm not suggesting to you that -- well, all I'm trying to explain is how an individual Adam's size would have gotten into the culvert, and people are all sizes. So that's what we believe happened. I'd like to just speak a little bit about why the water was there next and sort out the events that led up to this particular tragedy."

"Just before you go on, Mr. Pearson, with respect to the drawing, you said that the dugout area where the culvert in question was 20 feet long?" Judge Guy asked.

"Approximately."

"And how wide would it have been at that point?"

Pearson replied, "Just looking at this, I would -- I think this is roughly to scale and I would say, you know, it varies, but say 6 to 8 feet, depending on location."

"And based on your drawing there you would agree then -- or from prior evidence that at the time of this accident the culvert in question would not have been visible?"

"The culvert was under water at the time and the evidence -- or the -- I shouldn't say evidence. The information that we have is that there was a vortex that was present off and on. That's not unusual with vortices. A vortex is created when you have what we call non-symmetrical flow towards a pipe and it tends to cause a swirl to occur and they tend to submerge from time to time so you may not see it from the surface but it may still be there. In addition, if there were debris or snow or whatever going through there at the same time, that would tend to realign the flow and you may see the thing just sort of come and go. It's not as consistent as you might see, for example, in your sink, you know, when you have a vortex."

Kelly continued, "So it's conceivable at the time of the incident that the water would have been calm on top?"

"It may have been calm off and on. From the information that we have, there was a piece of styrofoam in a vortex so, you know..."

"I just want you to take a look at this if you would, Sir. This has been marked as Exhibit "A" for identification, and perhaps at this point, it would be appropriate if you would be able to identify those photos."

"Yes," Pearson replied, "I asked a member of our staff to take those photos just recently and what they show is three bars through the culvert, two of which were installed by our staff and a third one which was installed by somebody else."

Pearson wasn't going to identify the somebody else. It was Kevin and I.

"And just for informational purposes, the width of that culvert, I see you had a tape measure in there."

"Yes."

"And the width of that culvert?"

"Is 16 inches."

Prior to the calling of the inquest, in the letter to the Justice Department, Pearson claimed it was 14 inches.

Kelly asked, "That's the opening, right?"

"That's the clear opening across the culvert, yes."

"And, in fact, that's the culvert where the accident occurred?"

"That is the culvert, yes, Sir."

"Okay. We'll talk about the bars a bit later."

"Yeah."

Pearson went on, using several charts showing snow accumulation and temperatures, as well as talking about the drainage in the area. He placed most of the emphasis on these facts.

Judge Guy was getting impatient. "Well, but that -- tell me how that relates to the culvert, or does it relate to the culvert?"

Pearson thought for a moment. " It doesn't relate to the culvert."

"Okay. So that's the basement flooding and that kind of thing," Guy replied.

"That's the basement flooding piece, yeah."

"That's interesting," Guy said, "but not relevant to that extent, from my point of view."

A few moments later, after some talk about the different sewer systems, Pearson reached for another drawing. "This drawing that you see here is a plan and what we call a profile or sectional view looking through the catch basin and the culvert that existed -- or that exists on Leila where Adam Young was drowned, and it describes, in more detail, what we have seen on the other drawings."

"And for orientation purposes, this manhole which you see a sectional view here, and this is the same manhole in plan, is the manhole in the roadway. And we know that on the day that this happened that manhole was under water. There was a very shallow layer of water over the road and that extended along the ditch. And as I said earlier, there was roughly a foot or so of water in the shallow portion of the -- of the ditch and then about a metre or so, waist deep, in the deeper section adjoining the culvert. So again, this shows -- there's a waste water sewer, manhole, that's in the ditch, in the deep portion. That's this fellow right here, and there's the land drainage manhole. This is the deep part of the ditch where the culvert was installed. There's the culvert running into the manhole. It shows in section here. It's important to recognize that it is sloped and the slope is about -- well, it's 15.7 percent and to translate that, that means that in a reach of a 100 inches it would rise or decline, depending on which way you're looking at it, 15.7 inches. Roughly 8 inches in 4 feet. So it's sloping. It's not a steep slope in the context of, you know, walking up and down something but in the hydraulic context. It's important because it changes the flow regime in the culvert and changes it from a conventional culvert to one that is what we call "in limiting", and that's why we had such high flows in the culvert was because of the slope."

"On the day in question we had, according to records, water up to just above the top of the land drainage sewer which discharges from the manhole and just -- by the way, this is a 400 culvert. That's 16 inches. This land drainage sewer is 600. That's about 2 feet. This manhole is 230 -- let's see, about 1.75 metres deep. It's not a
very deep manhole at all. Very shallow. Most people could stand in that and look out the top. I probably couldn't, but most people could. Where you see the circle here going that way into the paper and on plan here is a land drainage sewer from the school that drains the parking lot. So we had a condition, as I said earlier, where there was a bit of a vortex here, about a 6 inch vortex, in proximity to this inlet."

Pearson continued, "Velocities in the ditch would be variable, depending on how close you got to this inlet. The closer you get the higher the velocities. And as we said earlier, Adam Young would have been drawn in feet first. This land drainage sewer is exactly aligned with the inlet culvert, so we hypothesized that he would have just been carried straight through the manhole."

"On that point, the flow being as high as it was, in the absence of any -- anything that would have kept him from going down the pipe, he would have been a long way away from this location very quickly. You know, in a matter of minutes he would have been down at Leila -- or sorry, Manila and Jefferson. So although the fire department responded very quickly, our guess is that he was well down the pipe at that time."

"The fellow who was caught on the pipe here had his legs, from what we understand, hooked around here. They had difficulty removing him. That's not surprising given that they were trying to pull him up. They weren't aware of the configuration of the pipe and I believe that he was fairly secure except that he was in very cold water and if he had succumbed to that, he would have been in the same tragedy that Adam Young was," Pearson said without emotion.

He just kept going on. This was more like a sales presentation than a testimony. "I'd like to talk a bit about why this is where it is. The -- we -- I have to refer to my notes for this."

After checking his notes, Pearson continued, "This land drainage sewer extension was built to facilitate the construction of the new school that we spoke of earlier. We -- and it was funded by the school. We received a drawing from Lombard North who were engaged by the school in July of 1989, and that particular drawing indicates," Pearson paused and looked down. "Well," he raised his head and paused again, "it doesn't indicate what's here. This inlet culvert was not depicted in that proposal."

"What they proposed was simply to - I'm referring to Exhibit 13 now - they proposed to have a land drainage manhole here and the sewer running up and a cross culvert in the driveway so that the drainage from this ditch would run through the cross culvert and be picked up by the existing catch basin in the ditch. That was excellent at that time in '89. So the culvert that you see here was not proposed."

"The -- subsequent to that in, I believe September '94 we --

our people were driving around inspecting things and determined that there was some construction going on here. They contacted Lombard North, who were responsible for the site development, as I understand, for the school, to discuss what was happening because we had received no final drawings for approval. At that time there was some discussions between Lombard North and the then -- then district engineer and his assistant relative to this matter and Lombard North expanded the terms of reference for their work to retain a consultant firm, S.E.G. Engineering, to undertake the municipal design of this system, and they did that at the City of Winnipeg's request. It is our standard to require that these types of works be designed and the supervision of the construction be undertaken by an engineer who is qualified in that field of work and that's what we did."

He continued, quietly, "During the course of construction they determined that there was a misalignment of this piping system and there was some problem with the position of the cross culvert here relative to the location where the manhole was supposed to go, and the consultant made a field decision based on that to relocate the manhole and to install the culvert as we see it on this drawing. That was done without any authorization by the City of Winnipeg."

Again, Pearson lowered his head, "That would not be normal -- or would not be unusual, I should say, simply because we rely on the design professional to make those kinds of decisions."

"However," he seemed like he didn't want to go on, "we did do a final inspection of these works, and that was undertaken for the purposes of ensuring conformance to the engineer's design and what standards we do have governing these types of things, and there was, you know -- there was some minor problems with grouting and the like but nothing significant that was identified. So that's how this ended up where it is, according to our records."

This was the first time any of us had heard this. For five months the city had kept this a secret. They didn't authorize it, but they approved it. They knew this could be dangerous from the moment they saw it. For four years, this hole was lying in the school ground waiting. Waiting for this to happen.

"Maybe at this point, Mr. Pearson," Kelly said, "it would be appropriate if you would actually talk about the issue of standards with respect to the City of Winnipeg and its standards on installation of those type of instruments."

"Sure. We have standards for many things. We have a book several inches thick of standards. We do not have standards relating to inlet safety of culverts. What we do in that instance, as we do with many other things, is we rely on the expertise of the design professional that's been engaged to ensure that the -- whatever is being designed is safe. That's not -- and that may or may not be referenced in the terms of reference that the -- that the professional is engaged under, and I don't -- I'm not privy to the terms of reference that Solvenson were engaged under because they worked for Lombard North who worked for the school division. But to -- I guess to put it bluntly, to say that you had to tell an engineer to make sure something is safe would be analogous to telling a doctor not to kill a patient. Our cannons are quite clear. I have a copy of the professional engineer's code of ethics, the fundamental cannons, and the second one on the list right behind obeying the laws of the land is: A professional engineer shall regard the physical, economic and environmental well being of the public as the prime responsibility in all aspects of engineering work."

Pearson placed the book down and continued, "So from our perspective, when we retain a professional with experience in these types of things it's implicit that there's an expectation that they will be designed and constructed in a safe manner."

Judge Guy looked confused, "But let me see if I understand this. This was still -- is there something unsafe about this? Is this something that you wouldn't have done? I guess I'm trying to find the relevancy of your last bit of testimony with respect to -- I guess I'm not concerned about who did it or that kind of thing. If it was done -- if it wasn't done properly, someone should have done it properly.

"Yes," Pearson replied.

"Or shouldn't have approved it, should have changed it, but if it was done properly or satisfactorily then, so be it, it's there," Guy said.

"Yeah," Pearson replied. "From our perspective -- I'm trying to think of an appropriate way to answer this."

He paused for a moment before answering, " We have -- we have about 175 or 200 similar installations throughout the city so -- and each of these is different in some respect. That's why -- that's one of the reasons why I believe that there are no standards, because these have to be examined in the situational context."

"I would say that this does not pose an obvious -- in the absence of the experience that we've had with respect to Adam Young, this would not be an obvious safety hazard. Having said that, we have done considerable work subsequent to this to ensure that it doesn't happen in other locations," Pearson said.

"The other thing I would say is that from a technical perspective there are more optimum solutions to this problem that prevent debris from getting into the system, and there is a problem with this type of design from that perspective because there's no, you know -- a typical catch basin has a location where debris can be caught and it keeps it out of the system. In fact we are aware from the Monday prior to the accident that there was some debris in the manhole So, you know, from a technical perspective, it's not optimum but it's something, as I said, that has been done in almost 200 other locations that I'm aware of."

Kelly looked at Pearson, "With respect to the standards, let's see if I understand this. The City, in general, has no directive set in terms of how these things are developed and attached to the City system?"

"That's correct."

"But what the City requires is that before -- for example, with the school here, before the City would allow such to happen that they would connect their drainage systems to the main sewer lines is that the City has to retain a consultant -- an engineer, a civil engineer and propose plans on how they would do that?"

"Yes."

"Those are submitted to the City and either approved or alterations ordered or whatever."

"Um-hmm."

"And it's all done in blocks, i.e., is that if the school wanted to do something they would submit a plan; if the guy next door wanted to do something - like the fire hall - they would submit a plan on how to connect?"

"Yeah. The submittals are consistent with the development. For example Amber Trails, Gen-Star would have submitted a plan, a master plan, for that whole area at the time that was developed."

Kelly asked, "And the issue is for the City in terms of looking at it is if they are, for lack of a better word, mechanically correct so that they will achieve the end result. The issue of safety for the instrument itself is not specifically addressed by the City per se, with guidelines or anything; you rely on the cannons?"

"In this case there are standards. I'd just like to mention we do have standards, for example, for a catch basin grates and there is a reason for that. That reason is that from an inventory perspective, we want to standardize, and they will have such things as size and grate spacing. That spacing is set to keep bicycles from getting caught in them, you know. So we do have standards for some elements and not for others and -- in any event, the application of our standards in a safe manner would be the responsibility of the professional."

"So the City doesn't set out standards that it expects the engineers to meet?"

"Not prescriptive standards, no," Pearson replied.

"Okay. Now, I think what His Honour was getting at with respect to this particular culvert is, in your opinion, is it at this point a safe."

"I was at that site the evening that Adam Young drowned and looking at it, I was surprised that the event could have occurred. Having said that, it did occur, and as a consequence of that, we have done a lot of work to protect similar installations and, you know, I think the answer is an accident happened, somebody died and, obviously, as a consequence, we have to say that it wasn't safe, said Pearson.

"That's fair. With respect, you say that the City has undertaken to do certain items."

"Yes."

"What is that exactly? What have they --"

"I should maybe sort of step back to the day in question and I can -- the incident occurred during the flood and there was very little we could do at the time. However, we did, through the media, request that people be aware of these types of things and stay away from them. There were other hazards out there as well, as you can imagine with open water and dikes and the army was in and there was a lot of traffic, so it wasn't a very safe place to be, Winnipeg, at that time. I should emphasize, you know, that this event was quite independent of the flood. However, it wasn't independent of the snow melt, but it was independent of the flood. So we got the word out to the media. We recognized that we couldn't do anything about it until after the flood, and staff were just -- they worked twelve hours a day for six weeks on the flood."

Pearson continued, "Early June things wound down and we started to look at the system. We have what we call a LAN-based information system, which is a computer based series of maps that we use to record our inventory, and it was our hope that we could use that to identify where these types of installations were."

"We tried to do that. That information is not configured in a fashion that makes it accessible; you can't extract it from the system, and in any event our inspection indicated that, in some cases, these things just aren't recorded on the system. Our system is quite old. It's evolved over time through a series of amalgamations predating Unicity and not all the records are there," he said.

"So about I guess the middle of June, after we did that, we came to the conclusion that we lacked the resources to properly inventory our system and to identify where these things were."

"We retained a consulting firm subsequent to that. We had discussions with the firm in June. We received approval to engage the firm - I don't have the exact date with me, but it would have been about the end of July I believe - and we had them, in fact, working on it in anticipation of approval because the clock was running and we wanted to get this stuff looked after."

Dave turned and looked over in my direction. I knew what he was thinking. If they had contacted this consultant, in June, why wasn't it mentioned in the report to the Medical Examiner's office? Why was this such a secret. We both knew the consultant was not engaged until after the inquest was called. Harry Lazarenko testified to that.

"We asked them to review the circumstances around the event. We asked them to identify similar locations and to recommend mitigative action. They visited, over the course of the summer, about 5,000 locations. At each location they documented the size of the installation, some of the physical characteristics, they photographed it and so forth. And they boiled that down to about 150 or so sites that, based on their review of the accident, on their review of other standards, they believed required attention. I'll just get my notes here."

Guy interrupted, "Perhaps this might be a time to break. I

guess my concern is that we do wrap up today for obvious reasons. Perhaps -- would 1:30 be convenient to all counsel so that we give yourself a better chance of doing that. So why don't we adjourn until 1:30 and that will give Mr. Pearson time to find his material.

At 1:30 Kelly Moar started. "Good afternoon, Your Honour. Continuing with Mr. Pearson, Your Honour. Just before we broke for recess the question posed to Mr. Pearson, which he was looking for his documents was, What, in fact, has the City been doing subsequent to this incident occurring, and Mr. Pearson, I understand, has found his documents and can proceed with that question.

Pearson said, "I think where we left off was I was describing the circumstances immediately after the accident in terms of our activities. And I guess to perhaps start, the first thing that happened, and it happened immediately after the accident, was that the site was secured, and there are photos, I believe, that you have seen already of that. Essentially, we erected a piece of chain link fencing immediately in front of the culvert and we drove in some steel rods or fence posts to keep that upright. We also erected a bit of a snow fence, a purple -- or sorry, orange snow fence around it, and that was done not in the context of safety per se but just to keep people away from it as much as we could. I may have mentioned before lunch that this occurred as the flood was transpiring. We didn't really get to the point where we could do much about it until June and, in fact, in early June we wrote a letter to the medical examiner who had asked us basically what had happened and what we were doing about it, and in that letter we indicated that immediately after the culvert -- or the accident, we secured the culvert. We also issued a directive to field staff, at that time, to be vigilant for similar types of installations and to report those so that we could take appropriate action if, in fact, there were any. We, as I mentioned earlier I believe, worked with the media relative to the matter of notifying the public."

Pearson continued, "We were also working with ourselves to try and locate Adam Young, and in that respect it took about ten days to locate his body. We -- we, on a daily basis, were examining our facilities. The -- in fact, we had a discussion with Mr. Young relative to this so that he would understand what we were doing immediately after the accident. But the sewer that we were discussing runs along over to Jefferson then back up to Leila and out to the river, it's a storm sewer so that it was, at that time of the accident, closed at this location because the river water was high and we didn't want it backing up into our system. However, there is a flood pumping station here, as well and a diversion chamber at Main Street. And so on a daily basis at a minimum we were popping the manholes all the way along here and going down and looking for Adam, as well as on a periodic basis de-watering the structures to locate him and finally, after ten days, he was found at this diversion here on Main Street.

"The photographs have been filed concerning that chamber," Judge Guy said. He had seen the pictures of Adam lying in the chamber.

"Okay," Pearson said. "I may have mentioned that we queried our LAN-based information system relative to identifying other locations. At the time we wrote the letter to the medical examiner, that hadn't been undertaken and we were optimistic that we would be able to, through that query, find these types of installations. We weren't able to and that was the reason we engaged the consulting firm. And really, that's the variation between what's in this letter and what happened subsequently because of the resource issue, we engaged a firm to undertake some of the work that we outline in the

letter and it took a lot longer than we had hoped it would, because rather than going through our computers we had to physically go to these 5,000 or so locations to identify the problems.

Samphir had discussed my testimony with Pearson during the break. They had to address it before Dave's cross examination.

Judge Guy asked, "We've heard some testimony about this consultant's report. Have you got the consultant's report now?"

"No," Pearson replied. "The consultant's report is not complete. It's a work in progress. The work that has been complete has been the examination of the sites and the review of standards in existence in other locales and recommendations specific to mitigation of the sites that were identified. There are other issues that we have asked the consultant to review that haven't been completed. And those ones that I've just discussed are available in draft form. We were focusing principally on the - I guess the task of under-

standing what happened with respect to the accident and identifying possible locations that need protection and getting that done before snow. From our perspective, these types of installations don't present an unusual hazard during the summer months. They do, by way of experience, appear to have that hazard associated with them in the
spring during the spring run-off. So we wanted to get these things identified and deal with them prior to the snow."

"I guess what has -- you've talked about examination, you've talked about recommendations. What has been done?" Judge Guy asked directly

"Well, what has been done is, based on the consultant's review - and I can speak to standards in a minute - but the consultant believes that the appropriate way to -- to make these safer is to install vertical bars at 6 inch centres and, in fact, that's been ongoing. The work started - that's what I was checking my notes for - I'm trying to locate a specific date, but it would have been in September, and our goal was to have basically all of them complete with the exception of some larger - there is eleven large ones we've identified. Our goal was to have them complete by about the 15th of this month to provide some leeway relative to the weather. We have completed all of the -- I believe if we haven't, we're close to completing all the ones that have been identified. We have found another 25 or so through the course of this work. And the type of installation that is being done is shown on these photographs..."

"Okay. These photographs, I apologize I haven't got these on a board or anything, but this would show a 200 diameter. That's about a 10 inch pipe and that pipe," Pearson was holding and pointing to photographs. "That particular bar is vertical. This would be - -"

Judge Guy looked at Pearson's pictures, "You mentioned before "vertical bar 6 inch centre"."

"Yes."

"And does that -- you said -- how broad is this? How wide?"

"That would be 10 inches."

"Okay. And does 6 inch centre mean -- means what?"

"Based on the consultant's review of the American Society of Civil Engineer's documents in other jurisdictions it's believed that a 6 inch centre is -- is adequate to prevent a child from passing through. The other I guess nuance is the orientation of the bar. The reason that the bars are oriented vertically rather than horizontally is that if, for example, an individual came against those bars and their arms were underneath them they would tend to be trapped. So the literature suggests that it's safer to have these things vertical so that you have the mobility to reach up and pull yourself away. For the smaller diameter culverts such as that one, a single bar suffices. For the larger ones -- this is a 400. This would be the same size as the one on Leila and, of course, because of the size it needs two bars. And of course --"

Guy interrupted, "Okay. Let me just -- so I'm absolutely clear on this. When you talk about the 6 inch centres, does that mean it can't be any larger opening than 6 inches?

"The space, centre to centre, on the bars should be 6 inches."

"Okay. Talk to me about that one," Guy asked as he pointed to one of the pictures.

"Okay. That's a 16 inch diameter culvert and it's been divided into three equidistant spaces, so they would be slightly less than 6 inches each. And if it were 18 inches, it would be the same. If it were 24 inch there would be three bars dividing it into four equidistant sections.

"Okay. So do I understand that it can't be more than 6 inches?"

"That's what the literature suggests and that's what we've been recommended.

"Okay," Guy said.

"Now, that's fine for the smaller pipes. And the other one, I just add, is there are locations where we determined that we have manholes and ditches that have been modified to facilitate drainage whereby somebody has pounded a hole in the side of it. And, again, if the size of that hole is large, we believed that it was appropriate to
protect that, and in those locations we're installing this type of a -- it's a pipe with a bar through it. I would add that not all of these locations, I believe if you were to analyze them hydraulically, would be seen to be of a similar circumstance to this. The fact is that it's more economical for us to protect them than it is to analyze them and it eliminates the risk. So these are the photos of what we've done. The specific -- the culvert on Leila, as I mentioned earlier,

was protected using chain link fencing and subsequently, I think it was on the 23rd of June, along with two other staff -- or two other locations our staff removed that chain link and installed bars in a criss-cross position."

Judge Guy glanced over his notes then looked to Pearson, "Can you tell me, and I know where we are with respect to the numbers that you received. You've mentioned there's eleven large ones."

"Yes," Pearson said.

"Today actually is the 15th of the month --"

Pearson interrupted. He knew what the question was. "Yeah. We've -- we've -- I spoke with our consultant this morning and he believed at the time that we were very close to completing all of the culverts and we had about 30 or 40 manholes to complete. And given the progress that we've seen to date, I don't believe there will be any difficulty in having that done before winter. The eleven that I mentioned that are larger pose some different types of problems. Again, based on our assessment and advice we've received, they have to -- they require some engineering analysis. If -- for example, if you take a 4 foot in diameter culvert with a lot of flow through it and you install these bars in a vertical orientation, it may well be that during a high flow condition an individual could be swept against the bars and be pinned by the current. So -- and there are other issues such as hydraulics and cleaning that have to be considered, so they will require likely some structural work. And our objective with respect to those is to undertake the necessary engineering analysis and get those completed over the winter so that they are protected by next spring. That will require an allocation of resources and we don't know what those resources will be until we have a solution. So it may be that we'll have to obtain funding for that but I don't anticipate any problem with getting that funding. So that's where that sits."

"Maybe, Mr. Pearson, if you wouldn't mind, you indicated there were engine -- or the consultant undertook to contact other jurisdictions to see if there were standards in existence," Kelly requested.

"We -- the consultant called, let's see -- I'll just read them off: Brandon, Regina, Saskatoon, Calgary, Edmonton, the Vancouver region, which included various jurisdictions including Chiliwack,

Burnaby, Delta and Indian Affairs Canada for the B.C. region, and Ontario. And stepping through them: Brandon does not have a specific standard in their design manual and they have indicated that the need for inlet safety grating is established on a case-by-case basis, according to the site needs."

"Regina, similarly, do not have overall standards. They do require that culverts over 900 millimetres in diameter, which would be approximately 3 feet, be protected with inlet safety grating, and the concern that they have with respect to that is unauthorized access via the outlets of the system, and people tend to want to crawl into these things and sometimes they actually live in them. It's just the way things go these days."

"Saskatoon similarly were not addressed by overall standards and they are assessed on a case-by-case basis. They have indicated that it's uncommon to protect culverts less than 600 millimetres in diameter. 600 would be about 2 feet in diameter. This particular one is 400."

"Calgary have indicated that they are not addressed by design standards. The same remarks basically as Saskatoon, case-by-case, uncommon less than 600, and site specific design."

"Edmonton similarly -- Edmonton has a clause in their design standards suggesting that the practitioner should examine safety. They don't have a specific standard and, again, case by case."

"Vancouver require gratings where egress is restricted by an outlet trash grating. So they would suggest that if -- or in a case like this, where there is restricted egress, they would look for a -- for a inlet protector. However, the requirement is typically applied to culverts, in one case in excess of 525 millimetres and in another case,
in excess of 600. It varies depending upon the community within the region."

"INAQ Western Region for B.C. have a clause which says, Where outlet is submerged or access to inlet is possible provide protection by grating. So it's left to the discretion."

Judge Guy asked, "So in summary, it appears in other jurisdictions it's done by a case-by-case basis. There's a lack of standards and if it's over a certain amount, the diameter is the most important feature whether they do it or don't.

Pearson replied, "Yeah. And the smallest one we found was

Ontario where it's 450. Now, having said that, there is a publication, it's a reference material for guidance. It's used by guidance -- as guidance by practitioners, called the American Society of Civil Engineer's Manual, and it -- I'll just see if I can locate that." Pearson
picked up his book. "It's prepared by a U.S. based organization. It's really a North American organization, in essence though, but the -- the forward is carefully crafted to place the responsibility for these things on the individual designers, not to be seen as an absolute. And it says:

> Culverts normally run short distances beneath roads, et cetera. In cases where drainage ditches transition to drainage pipes that run for hundreds or even thousands of feet, as is common in the midwest, a safety rack at the pipe entrance is recommended because of consequences of debris blockage within the pipe and for public safety.

"So that's the other standard that we've seen. It doesn't reference a size and again, it leaves that to the discretion of the practitioner."

"So we, based on this information and weighing the cost of protecting these versus analyzing them, elected to protect them all. We recognize that will result in some additional problems, as a consequence, relative to blockage of these things during spring run-off and rainfall, however, we saw the balance as being in favour of being cautious rather than being concerned about the drainage."

"You've indicated some of the things that the consultant report has given you already, specifically with respect to these culverts, is there anything else that you've asked of the consultant firm that the Court should be aware of?" Judge Guy asked.

"Let me just check my notes and I can tell you what we did ask the consultant to do. The specifics that we requested of the consultant were: An assessment as to the cause of the accident so that other portions of the City's drainage system that could pose a similar risk in terms of the public's exposure/access to City-owned lands could be identified; the development of a comprehensive inventory of all locations where open-ended inlets exist that are directly connected to a closed conduit drainage system or whose discharge point may pose a similar risk in terms of compromising public safety; recommendations on what measures should be undertaken in the short-term to eliminate this risk or mitigate it to an acceptable level.

And finally: a review of current design standards as they relate to inlet safety and the provision of recommendations on appropriate design standards for the long-term."

"So I suppose the one issue that we haven't covered is --."

Judge Guy stopped Pearson. He looked at him, "Can you just give me the date of that letter, too, please."

"I'm sorry, that's not a letter, it's an excerpt from the consultant's proposal," Pearson replied.

"Oh, I see. Okay."

"I don't have a date on it. But we can get that if it's important. We -- that's the one thing we haven't discussed and that's something that's still open from the consultant's perspective and that is whether we should be more prescriptive with respect to our current standards. In other words, should we direct the professional to do certain things or should we just ask them to consider certain things in the application of their knowledge to design something. My guess is that we will likely be proposing to council that this type of installation be replaced with a different type of engineered, high capacity inlet structure which can deal with issues associated with trash removal in a fairly efficient manner as well as being protected by bars to keep people out of it. However, that remains to be determined," said Pearson.

Kelly was still standing. He looked at Pearson, "I think that just on that point, this is the City's -- or maybe I'll ask, in your opinion -- or is it your department's intention, with respect to any future culverts that are built, that safety standards be actually incorporated as a policy within the City rather than being left to the individual engineers themselves?

Pearson said, "I believe that it's appropriate to remind the professional of their responsibility to ensure that the thing is safe and I believe that it's appropriate for us to -- as an organization, to steer them away from this type of a thing and look at a more complex costly structure which will have the benefits of keeping foreign material out of the system as well as being safer. So that's -- I think that's where we'll end up going. I think it's important, however, not to tie the professional's hands with respect to applying their knowledge and skills to provide the best possible solution."

"With reference to the culverts themselves, as you've indicated, you have left it to the consultants to design these and safety is supposed to be a factor. Are you aware of any consulting firms or engineers that actually incorporate grids as a standard feature when they built these?" Kelly asked.

"We have, because of the size of our system, a wide variation of installations and certainly, we have some in the 3 foot diameter range that are protected and we have some that aren't right now. The inlet hydraulics play an important role there, and also relative location of the thing, whether it's in the City or whether it's out in no man's land are important. So we -- we've got both right now."

Kelly continued, "The reason that I ask that is that earlier in -- when Mr. Young testified, in his testimony he indicated there were numerous culverts in areas that are populated by daycares and/or schools and the concern, I think, from that perspective is whether or not the City is going to take the stance that those type of installations have to be grated in order for protection."

"Oh, those," Pearson said, "if they fall into the category that we've spoken of here, they will be protected. They are either on our list to be protected or if they aren't we would like to know of them. And I believe that there was one reference on Waverly and some out on Haney, those are on our list now, and were on our list and they -- if they haven't been looked after by today, they certainly will be before there is snow on the ground."

Judge Guy stared at Pearson, "Well, I don't think it matters whether my child is in danger next to his school or he's in danger on his way home."

Pearson replied quietly, "Yeah."

Kelly said, "Well, I think there's higher danger areas associated that have to be addressed immediately."

Pearson replied, "I should emphasize that we spent a lot of time, effort, and money to try and find all of these. It was a large task and if we have missed them it's not because we haven't looked for them. Having said that, there is a probability that we haven't found them all and that means we will continue to look for them. We've done, I think with our resources, the best we can."

"Okay," Kelly said. He turned to the judge. "Those are the questions I have for Mr. Pearson.

Judge Guy turned to Dave, "Okay. Mr. Guttman."

Dave stood and turned to Pearson, "Would you like a break, Mr. Pearson, before we begin?"

"I wouldn't mind a glass of water."

The court clerk handed Tom a glass of water. Dave waited for Pearson to finish.

"Mr. Pearson, firstly, I wonder if you have the draft report from the consultant with you?"

"No, I don't." Pearson paused. "I have sections of the report. It doesn't exist in total yet and they've been working on it on a piecemeal basis, and the sections I have are likely undergoing revisions as we speak."

"Are you prepared to have the sections that you brought with you entered as an exhibit in these proceedings?"

Pearson replied, "Given that they are undergoing revision I -- I wonder whether it would be appropriate. I'm not qualified to really comment on that.

Judge Guy asked Dave, "Do you need them for some reason?"

Dave replied, "At least the recommendations, I think, should be an exhibit, Your Honour."

Judge Guy checked his notes, "Well, they are on the record. He's given what the recommendations are. They are on the record."

For some time the City made comments about this report. Various officials had commented that it was completed, some denied it's existence. Dave was trying to find out what the truth was.

"I believe he's read part of it," Dave said. "I don't believe he read the entire page."

Samphir jumped up, "Well, at this point in time, we're not prepared to submit the draft report. That's --"

"Well, I'm not interested in the draft report and I'm only interested in what interests me here now," Judge Guy responded angrily.

The inquest was called to determine the circumstances surrounding Adam's death, not for the discovery of a cover-up. We all knew that. What Dave was trying to do with this opportunity to rehearse for a possible lawsuit or maybe scare them enough to start taking responsibility. We felt that this report never existed. Judge Guy knew what Dave was doing. He also realized this was not the forum.

"That's what -," Marvin was still on his feet.

Judge Guy asked Pearson, "The recommendations, did you read all the recommendations given by the engineer?"

Pearson replied, "I'm not certain what you mean by recommendations."

Judge Guy wanted a straight answer. "Well, my understanding is you read -- when I asked you about the engineering report you read --,"

Pearson said, "The things that they were to do for us."

"Yes. Did you read all of them?"

"Yes, I did.

"Yeah, all that was on that page?"

"All of the items that were bullets, yeah," Pearson said.

"Okay," Guy said, "Thank you."

Dave was still standing, "That was the proposal. However, the recommendations themselves, I don't believe they were all completely read in. Perhaps I'm mistaken. You can show me."

"I didn't read recommendations. I spoke to recommendations which are contained in tabular form relative," Pearson stopped, "actually, they weren't recommendations either. They were standards of other jurisdictions. I do not have recommendations with me."

Dave asked, "Do you have notes as to the recommendations with you?"

"Other than what's in the record, I have nothing further to offer."

Dave made his point. He continued, " Okay. With respect to the standards, could I see those, the notes you had on them or the chart, whatever the case may be. And this is prepared by who?"

Pearson replied, "This was prepared by our consultant, that's UMA Engineering. Their office is in Winnipeg on Buffalo Place."

"Do we know on what basis they did this research, whether they dealt with all culverts or whether they dealt specifically only with culverts that attached to drainage systems?"

"I suspect that they would have described the circumstances surrounding this incident and requested information relative to that. There would certainly be no reason for them to, for example, discuss culverts, whether they be large or small, under a roadway or a driveway because those are simply not hazardous installations in the connotations that we're talking about today."

"But you don't actually know what they did; you just have this response; is that right?"

"I wasn't -- I wasn't -- I requested that work be done according to the terms of reference and I assume that that's what they did."

Dave wasn't going to let go of this. He continued, "Now, you indicated earlier in an answer to a question by His Honour that you could advise as to the date of the letter to the consultant. Can you please advise us at this point?"

"Now, you're talking about the -- which letter?"

"The letter of retention and the letter telling them what you wanted them to do."

"The -- as my records show, we undertook discussions with the consultant in June. They began work on an informal basis in July in anticipation of an award. These things require approvals, and we directed that they begin immediately in anticipation of that approval, and that approval was provided by the Board of Commissioners and they were engaged on July 31st of '97. They, by the way, would have incurred significant cost by then."

"Would you agree with me, Sir, that no overtures were made to this consultant until after this inquest was called in mid to late June?," Dave asked.

"No. No, I wouldn't. I believe the inquest was called - I don't have that here.

"I believe it was June the 20th," Dave provided the answer.

"We were under discussion with the consultant, according to the information I have here, in mid June."

"Okay then, is there some reason why you didn't advise the medical examiners of that when you wrote to them back on the 11th of June?"

"Because we hadn't," Pearson stuttered. He was looking to Samphir, "we were -- at that point in time, we weren't contemplating engaging a consultant. We made that decision after we attempted to retain that -- or to get the information we needed from our LBIS system and we weren't able to, and then we realized that we'd better get some help to make this happen. The discussions we undertook in June were of a nature of determining that the firm had

the resources and the necessary qualifications to do the work. They were not specific to -- to what would be done. That came in July and, of
course, that's all required in anticipation of a report to the board to get the authorization and funding."

"When you wrote to Jim Hull," Dave asked, " back on the 11th of June, I believe your letter and diagram has already been marked as an exhibit, the diagram attached, who was that drawn by?"

"That was drawn by a graphic artist," Pearson said. "Or I'm not sure that's the right term for him. He's a fellow with artistic capabilities within our office. And it was done sometime prior to that, in fact, immediately after the accident before we, you know, before the water had actually subsided and it was done to try and convey to the media the nature of the installation that existed so that people would be aware of the hazards associated with that. It was not intended to be sort of a detailed description of that installation, and I would rely on the drawing that's before you as an exhibit there for that information."

The drawing was never meant for the media or the public. That was stated in the letter. It was not be released to anyone outside the Medical Examiner's office. This was indicated in a disclaimer in the actual report.

Dave continued, "Well, certainly I'm much more accepting of the drawing that's before us because it shows the slope and this drawing that was included in your letter to the medical examiner shows no slope to this particular pipe at all."

"That's right. As I say, it was prepared before we had the opportunity to examine the pipe and, accordingly, we weren't aware of that at the time."

Adam died April 21. The letter and the drawing are dated June 11, almost 2 months after the accident and they still had not examined the culvert.

"And you're quite accurate that the slope has an important bearing on the hydraulic capacity of the installation," Pearson replied.

"In your letter, you indicated that a directive was issued to field staff who maintained the land drainage system to locate and secure any similar installations," Dave stated. "Do you have a copy of that directive to provide to us?"

"I don't have it with me. It's certainly available. I believe it would have been in either a memorandum or electronic mail form."

"Okay." One by one, Dave was trying to discredit Pearson's earlier testimony.

"You also indicate you were informed that one such installation was subsequently identified and made secure. Can you tell us where that was?"

"I don't have that location but, again, if that's important to this inquest, we can get it."

"Okay. You indicated in your letter that as of June 11th you've already queried your LAN-based information system and you only identified three culverts at that point in time. You then say that it will involve the installing of bars. You say that there may be additional culverts not identified and that drawings will be reviewed. At that point, you don't talk about engaging a consultant in any way, but you're telling us that before that, you had already started inquiries."

Samphir tried to rescue his witness, "He didn't say before that."

Pearson said, "No, I didn't say that. I said that subsequent to that we made the decision based on the fact that we could not get the information from the LBIS system and through a review of our drawings that we lacked the resources to do the work and subsequently we started to talk to consultants."

"Is there some reason why this waited until June, why you wouldn't have been talking to consultants in late April or early May and making efforts to identify other sites at that point in time if, as we're told today, you've now identified, through a consultant, 175 of these sites?"

"The reason is quite simply resources at the time. I and everybody who works for me, all 250 of them, were working about twelve hours a day, seven days a week, trying to prevent your home from flooding and we did not have the time, albeit it's an important issue, to direct to this," Pearson yelled angrily.

Dave grinned, "Nonetheless, private consulting firms and engineering firms weren't necessarily as overworked as your department."

"I would take exception with that observation. Virtually, every contractor and consultant that we would have normally engaged was working on the flood through that period."

"Well, did you make efforts prior to June to engage anybody to assist in this?"

"Before June, I saw no need to. I expected that we would be able to do that using our own resources. As time permitted."

Now, you indicate that new installations," Dave said, "in your letter to Mr. Hull, should be designed with inlet protection. But what you're telling us today is that hasn't been done; is that fair?"

"I don't understand the question," Pearson replied.

"There's no standard in place right now that requires that inlet protection be provided, grading or bars or anything of that nature to new installations; is that fair?"

"We have not developed a standard as yet and we may or may not," Pearson stated. Dave was getting to him.

"And why is that?

"Because it's the design professional's responsibility to do that and there is an issue of liability if we tell them how to do their job. Having said that, we believe it's important that they understand their duty in that respect and certainly, that will be reflected in future terms of reference if, indeed, we elect not to prescribe solutions."

"Do you not agree that this situation that resulted in the death of this child was dangerous, was a hazard? Do you not agree with that, Sir?"

"I agree that there was a tragedy and certainly, I think it's fairly obvious that the fact that Adam Young was drowned means that that culvert was dangerous. I can't see how anybody could argue that."

"And is it your position, Sir, that the responsibility for that rests with the designer of this particular culvert as you seemed to hint at when you were speaking earlier?"

Judge Guy stepped in, "I don't think he hinted at that at all."

Dave responded, "Well, I think he hinted at the design professional and his responsibility."

Pearson said, "I can't speak to what considerations the individual that designed this took into account at the time. Certainly -- and accordingly, I can't -- I cannot say whether or not he discharged his responsibilities in an appropriate manner. That's something you would have to ask that individual."

Dave went on. "Okay. The City is the one that's responsible for maintaining and cleaning these particular types of installations; is that fair?"

"Yes."

"The City is responsible for inspecting these installations before they are allowed to proceed; is that fair?"

"To the extent that we inspect them for conformance to standards and material specifications, yes. We would expect that the design professional would have a responsibility to ensure that their design concept was built and functioning as they saw it to be appropriate."

"Would you agree with me that if, in fact, there had been a cover or bars on this particular pipe Adam Young would still be with us?"

"I believe that if it were done properly, he would be. And by that I mean similar to what we are proposing at the present time in doing."

"And, in fact," Dave said, "there was no purpose in having no cover on there because that particular pipe clogged repeatedly. We've heard evidence from the worker that, in fact, he was there the day before and prior to that unclogging it, steaming it, calling for the sewer department to help. What was the purpose in having it uncovered?

"The reality is, and I'm sure we will find this next spring," Pearson replied, "that the frequency of plugging will be considerably higher with the -- with the bars that we're putting in place than the open culvert that existed and I don't know the exact nature of the plugging that was a problem. Certainly, one of the problems we have with culverts through the spring is freezing and thawing and if it freezes it's going to plug; that's pretty fundamental. However, as soon as you introduce an obstruction in a culvert I can guarantee you that it will be more prone to plugging as a result of trash and that, as a consequence, there will be a higher level of overland flooding and other associated land drainage problems, and that's what we weigh in making these types of decisions."

"Are you telling me that somebody, at some point, considered putting a cover on this and decided not to? You're not saying that, are you, Sir? Dave asked with a grin.

"No, I'm not."

"Okay. My understanding is that the blockage that occurred and was removed at the manhole near this particular pipe was cement blocks. Pieces of cement blocks had, in fact, blocked the area; were you aware of that?"

"That's what our records show," Pearson replied.

"Okay. Do you have a report from your department as to what happened in the days leading up to this and the analysis of what took place on April 22nd?"

"No, I don't. Our consultant has spoken to a number of staff as well as reviewing the reports that I believe are in evidence in trying to come to some conclusions as to what happened, but I don't have a comprehensive report.

"Are you telling me your department didn't try to reconstruct what happened without the benefit of the consultant during the two or three months before you hired the consultant? Do we not have an overall report from your department as to what happened?"

"That's why we engaged the consultant or one of the reasons. I think I mentioned that in -- in speaking to the question."

"Are you intending to make this consultant's report public when it's finalized?"

"That will not be my decision."

"You had some meetings with Mr. Young; is that correct?"

"I met with Mr. Young the day after the incident along with Councillor O'Shaughnessy because we were aware that the media had a large interest in this and we felt it inappropriate to speak with the media until such time as we had spoken to Mr. Young to explain what had happened and subsequently, I believe I encountered Mr. Young in our office one day looking for standards. I don't have notes on either of those. I'm aware that the first meeting took place on April 23rd; the second one I can't pinpoint in terms of time."

"Can you tell us," Dave asked, "what was discussed between Councillor O'Shaughnessy and Mr. Young and yourself on April 23rd about remedying this type of dangerous situation?"

"I kept no notes of that meeting," Pearson stated, "and I would observe that it was quite stressful for all concerned. However, my recollection is that -- well, I'll just speak to what my objectives were in having the meeting and I think most of those were covered.

The first was to explain what had happened to Mr. Young's son, Adam in terms of where he might be and our efforts to locate him, and the second was to explain that there was little we could do other than warn people at the present -- at that time because of the issue of the flood and very severe resource issues we had as a result and finally, we spoke about the need to look after this problem and I undertook to have that happen, and that's, in essence, what we've been doing since then. I believe Councillor -- from my recollection Councillor O'Shaughnessy was similarly in favour of that step being taken. I suppose the final thing I asked of Mr. Young is that if he had any questions he call me and I provided a business card to him for that purpose."

"I believe Mr. Young also asked you for information concerning design and standards at the later meeting; is that correct?"

"He did request those."

"And, in fact, you didn't provide anything to him but instead sent him a letter indicating the material would be forwarded to his solicitor; is that fair?"

"Yeah, what happened at that stage was shortly thereafter we received a letter, it may have been from you, indicating an intent or a notice of intent to file suit and under the Freedom of Information Act, we at that stage had to be cautious about what we release and we did two things, we sent the letter and we requested advice of counsel relative to the matter."

"But, in fact, you indicated, and I'll quote," Dave held up Pearson's letter, "Accordingly, we will forward the information which we are compiling directly to your solicitor. And then it's signed by yourself. Do you recall that?"

"I remember that."

"Has any information been sent to me that you're aware of? By the City or by your department?"

"I believe that, as I said earlier, immediately thereafter we, at the department level, received a notice of intent relative to litigation and at that stage, the Freedom of Information by-law would preclude us from releasing information relative to the matter. At least that's the advice we would receive from our solicitor.

"So, in fact, the answer is "no"?"

Dave went on, "What troubles me is that there have been numerous promises to fix these things. How do we know that what you're telling us today has actually taken place?"

"You can look at the photographs or you can go out to one of the streets that's been remedied and examine that and certainly, if you have concerns, we'd be happy to discuss them."

"All right. I'm not attacking your personal integrity, Sir, but you're the head of a department, you're advised of certain things. My concern is that these things have actually taken place. Are you in a position to give His Honour a list of the sites and the date that the work was performed and photographs of each site that was repaired, not just the few photographs that were provided?"

"If that information is important to this inquest, we will provide it."

"And one thing that troubled me during your evidence was the fact that you've taken the position that there may be more that you don't know about."

"One of the things that I think we all have to understand is that we don't live in a perfect world. We have 10,000 kilometres of sewers to maintain, 400 kilometres of ditches, over a 100,000 catch basins. I can't sit here and tell you that we have found every one of these. I would be irresponsible if I did that."

"Well?" Dave glared at Pearson.

"Because I don't know that for a certainty."

"Well what you've told us, and correct me if I'm wrong, is that you hired this consultant and they photographed these 5,000 sites; is that true?"

"The consultant physically went to 5,000 sites based upon a fairly rigorous review of drawings and in order to come to the conclusion that these are possible sites where these things would have been."

"So what you're telling us is there may be one further site, there may be 15 further sites out there, and we don't know?"

Pearson dropped his head, "That's right."

Judge Guy replied, "Well -- yes. But how could we -- how could he say anything else, Counsellor?"

"I guess what I'm getting at is," Dave said, "what other measures is the City undertaking to ensure that the consultant has covered all of the affected areas? Are you engaged in any other procedures for looking for these or are you going to wait for complaints or for another incident to cause you to go forward?"

"We, in addition to having the consultant do their work, as we complete that phase will be engaging our own staff in a review of the system in concert with the consultant." Firstly, we will ask the consultant to review the sites that have been protected and ask staff whether -- whether they believe that there are some potential locations based upon the criteria that they have selected that have been overlooked."

Pearson continued, "Secondly, we will provide the staff with criteria and ask them, in the normal course of their duty, their day-to-day work, to be vigilant of these things and, finally, we will ask our partners, if you will, the consulting and construction industry, to exercise a similar level of vigilance so that we can, over time, hopefully identify any additional sites that exist. Those are some steps that we're taking and there may be others that we think of as this goes by, but those are the ones that come to mind right now."

"Okay. To be fair to you, Sir, I know that in April when you were interviewed by the police service, you told them all efforts would be made to have all these things fixed by the middle of June. And you simply didn't have the resources in which to do that; is that fair?"

"That's my assessment," Pearson stated.

"And you're not the individual who determines policy in your particular department. You simply assist in the implementation of it; is that correct?"

"Policy is set by Council. We recommend."

"And are your recommendations always followed?"

"I believe that where recommendations are appropriate they are followed by Council. Council has many things to balance and I would suggest to you that they would see this as an important issue."

"Okay. I think you've been fair and honest with us today. Is there any reason why members of Council were indicating to the public and their peers that the report from the consultant was complete almost a month ago?"

"I believe that was as a result of them not being aware of what was going on quite simply, and that's not their fault. We have a duty to keep them informed and obviously, we were not diligent in anticipating this question and providing the necessary information so that they could respond appropriately."

Councillor Bill Clement, when asked by Councillor Garth Steek, in the September Council Meeting, announced that the report was complete and he had read it. When Steek asked for a copy of it, Clement replied," I will have it on all the Councillor's desk by morning."

"And, Sir, in terms of the chain of command, who do you report to?"

"I report to the director of our department who reports to the Commissioner of Works and Operations."

Dave checked his notes quickly, then turned to Judge Guy. "Thank you very much. Those are my questions, Sir."

Judge Guy faced the city solicitor. "Any questions, Mr. Samphir?"

Samphir responded, "Could I have just a minute, please?"

After a few moments of checking his notes and whispering to his associate, Carswell, Samphir stood. "I believe everything has been covered. We have no questions to ask." He wasn't smiling.

19

"Ms. Paul, I understand that you are employed with the Seven Oaks School Division?" Kelly was questioning Linda Paul, the principal of the school.

"That's correct," she replied.

"And, in fact, my understanding is you were on April 22nd, 1997 the principal at the Ecole Leila North?"

"That's correct."

" And had you been at that school since it opened?"

"Yes, I had."

"And do you recall when the school opened?"

"In September of '92."

"And my understanding is you're no longer at that school?"

"No, I'm not."

"And when did you leave Ecole?"

"At the end of June of '97." Two months after Adam died, she was moved to a different school.

"Okay. So you had been there for approximately five years?"

"Yes."

"And you're now within the Seven Oaks School Division at another school?"

"That's correct."

"As you are obviously aware," Kelly said, "you're subpoenaed with respect to the issue of Adam Young's death. The site where Adam Young ultimately perished, are you aware of that site?"

"Yes, I am."

"Were you aware that there was a culvert at that site?"

"No, I was not."

"Let me backtrack a little bit now and ask you just some general issues. With respect to the school itself, does the school have a policy with respect to supervision of children?"

"Yes."

"Can you articulate the policy to His Honour."

Linda replied, "We supervise children inside the building and outside the building as it is deemed necessary for the age groups, so that we have some children that are supervised outside if it is thought necessary because of behaviours or physical or mental limitations. Inside the building, we have supervision. On field trips and things like that, we have normal supervision."

"Now, my understanding is that the school runs a -- or allows the children to eat lunch at school?"

"Yes, correct."

"During that period of time what, if any, supervision is provided to the children?"

"The lunchrooms are supervised," Paul said. "The hallways are supervised for the entire lunch hour."

"And with respect to the outside, the parameter of the school?"

"The -- there is outside supervision if certain children are outside."

"So it's target-specific with respect that supervision --"

"Yeah, that's right. The supervisors are target- specific but they do general supervision as well."

"Okay. So is it safe to say then that there's generally -- or there's not, say, two teachers outside that supervise the playground during the --"

"There would be -- they would not be teachers; they would be para-professionals."

"So if, in fact, these para-professionals, if their students weren't outside, there wouldn't be any supervision?

"Yes, that's right."

"So, in essence, they are responsible just for certain students, specifically?"

"Right," she replied.

Kelly continued asking Linda Paul questions. "Now, at the time of the lunch hour once a child leaves the school from lunch, can that child gain access to the school again?"

"Yes."

"So the doors are not locked at the school?"

"No, they are not."

Several parents were sitting in the gallery listening to Linda's testimony. They gasped when she responded to the question. We all knew the doors of the school were locked at lunch time. That's why the kids had to go to the firehall for help., they knew they couldn't gain access to school.

Kelly went on and asked general questions about the area. Linda did say the site where the culvert was located was not on school property.

"As a result of the accident," Kelly asked, "that happened with Adam Young, did the school take any additional precautions with respect to that area?

"No."

"No? Has the school, at any point, addressed the issue with students in terms of that area?"

"I can only speak for what we did in the springtime. I can't speak for what's happening now. The children -- there really wasn't very much of a need to address that because, really, it was an area that they didn't frequent after the accident.

"Okay. And again, you're not familiar of any incidents that occurred where parent's reported -- or civilians reported kids playing in the water in that area?"

"No, not to me they didn't."

"Has there ever been a time since you've been at the Ecole Leila North that there was general supervision provided of children during school hours?"

"No, not general supervision."

So that's never been --"

"No," she replied.

"I have no more questions." Kelly sat at his table.

Judge Guy looked over at Dave. "Mr. Guttman."

Dave stood, "Thank you, Your Honour."

"It's my understanding, Ms. Paul," Dave said, "that the supervision issue changed as a result of a collective agreement between the teachers and the school division; am I wrong in that?"

"Yes, you are."

"So you're telling me that at no time in the last five years were teachers supervising children outside the premises on lunch hours?"

"That's correct."

"That's your recollection?"

"Yes," she replied.

"And can I ask you whether or not you received a series of complaints from residents about children, not necessarily playing in water, but coming on their property and that type of thing? Do you recall that?"

"There would have been some complaints, yes."

"And how would you deal with those complaints?"

"We dealt with those individually as we knew the identity of the children. And we dealt with families if we knew, again, the identity of the children."

Dave asked, "Do you recall an incident involving the Young family and a gang of students that took place earlier in that same school year?"

"Not a gang of students, no."

"Do you recall a situation where you were contacted by the Young family and advised that two of the sons were being harassed by a group of other students?"

"I became aware that that had happened, yes."

"Were you not, in fact, spoken to by Rob Young and Kim Young about that?"

"I had not spoken to by Rob Young about that. I was spoken to by Kim about that, yes."

"And, in fact, did you take any action or did the Youngs' simply end up keeping their children at home for several days?"

"No, we took action."

"And what action did you take?"

"We asked that the children return to school so that we could mediate the situation between the children."

"And did that take place?"

"Yes, it did."

"And that was approximately ten days after it was first reported to you?"

"Approximately, yes." That was her way of dealing with issues. Ignore them long enough and they will go away. Linda didn't respond to this incident until after the police had been called. She addressed the issue with Adam and Kevin, not the gang that was harassing them. Two days after they returned to school, Kevin witnessed this gang beating a small Filipino boy, ten feet from the school doors, which of course were locked.

Dave let his point sit for a few minutes before continuing. "You had no concerns after what happened April 22nd that some of the other kids would get curious about this particular site and venture there?"

"The City had covered the site up after the accident had occurred. The vice-principal and I also had spent a lot of time outside on supervision ourselves after it occurred, frequently spending the lunch hours close to or at the site."

"Do you recall having a meeting with some of the other children who were present when Adam was sucked into the pipe?"

"Yes, I do."

"And do you recall blaming them for allowing this incident to happen at that time?"

"No, I do not."

"So it's your position, then, that you didn't exert any blame on any of the survivors?"

"That's correct."

"And if they say otherwise, they are mistaken?"

"That's correct."

One of Adam's friends had gone home crying the day after the accident. He told his parents about this meeting with the principal. He claimed that she blamed them for Adam's death. That it was their fault.

"Those are my questions," Dave finished and sat down at his table.

Judge Guy asked Samphir if he had any questions. Marvin declined.

Kelly stated to Judge Guy that he was calling his next witness. John Wiens. John was the superintendent of the School Division.

"Briefly, what does the job of superintendent entail?" Kelly asked.

Wien's replied, "I hold the position of superintendent and chief executive officer, two distinct roles. One of them is the educational leader of the school division; the second is the chief financial officer of the school division."

"Okay. Is part of your duties also to formulate policies within the school division?"

"Yes."

"Just prior to you, Sir, we had Ms. Pauls testifying with respect to the school, Leila North. Particularly, what I would like to ask, Sir, is, does the school -- or does the school division have any policy with respect to supervision of children during school hours?"

"We have no direct written policy. We are governed by the laws of the province and more specifically The Education and Administration Act, The Public Schools Act, and guidelines arising out of that Act called The Administrative, which are included in the administrative handbook for schools in Manitoba. So we have policy on discipline and general policy on supervision of field trips but during the school day, we are governed by policy according to the Acts."

"And what do those entail in terms of supervision? What do they tell you?"

"Well, the administrative handbook -- I could leave a copy here and I'll just maybe indicate to you it basically indicates that the school divisions are responsible for establishing supervision and discipline policies and procedures for their schools. Under that general kind of policy, I guess we have a policy that says principals are responsible for establishing guidelines and policies for all for their own schools. The policy itself states that there will be supervision commensurate - or something to the effect, at least of supervision commensurate with the age of the children."

"Now, Ecole Leila North School is grades 7 to 9, right?"

"Six to nine."

"Generally, we're looking at ages twelve to --"

"We have children as young as eleven and we have children as old as sixteen."

"Specifically for that school, what would be the policy in terms of supervision?"

"Specifically for that school, the policy would be that students would remain -- if they were bus students, they would remain in the school for a certain period of time during lunch period, and I'm not sure exactly what that is in terms of minutes. After which
they would be allowed to be -- allowed to remain in the school or they could leave the schoolyard if -- or leave the school building. If they left the school building they would be required to remain outside unless there was an emergency until such time as they could return."

"Okay. Once they left the building, would the building be locked or would it be open?"

"No, it would be open."

"And while they be outside during this time that they left during lunch hour, would there be any supervision outside for them provided by, say, the teachers?"

"In this school, and I might say as all our middle schools, the policy is basically the same, is that the students would know where they could find a supervisor which would generally be in or near the front of the school or at the office, depending on the location of the office."

"I remember when I went to school they would patrol the grounds. That no longer happens; is that safe to say?"

Wiens responded, "Well, yes and no. I think that it does happen if we have a student, for example, who is under immediate supervision at all times of the school day. That teacher, in one sense, also assumes responsibility for the area around, you know, where they are supervising, and that's always been the case. So the straight answer is no, okay, but --"

"There are some qualifications?"

"The qualification is that we might have supervisors for particular students who would supervise other parts."

"Another thing I want to ask you, Sir, I take it you are familiar with the site where the accident occurred with Mr. Young?"

"Yes, I am."

"In fact, my understanding is about four o'clock that afternoon of the accident, you attended?"

"I'm not sure. I think maybe it was earlier than that but it would be about that time, yes."

"Okay. Had you yourself, Sir, been made aware of the dangers of that area by any complaints being sent into the school division?"

"No. I was unaware that this was a dangerous site."

"That's the extent of my questions, Your Honour.

"Mr. Guttman," Guy said.

Dave stood, "Thank you, Your Honour. Mr. Wiens, we've heard some conflicting evidence as to what takes place over the lunch hour at Ecole Leila North. We heard from two students there that once they went outside after twelve o'clock, they weren't allowed back in the building until 12:50; is that accurate?"

Wiens replied, "They would probably not leave the school yard unless they are eating their lunch outside -- I should say the school itself. Unless they are eating their lunch outside, they would stay in the lunchroom for a period of time, fifteen to twenty minutes, probably at which time they would be supervised in the lunchroom. Once they had left the school, whether they went outside to eat their lunch or had left for any other reason, they would be required, in most instances, to stay outside unless there was an emergency."

"I understand that, but I think it's important here to determine whether or not the doors to the school were locked."

"Well, certainly it's not --"

"These children say that when they went outside to eat lunch, they could not get back into the school; that's what they have told us. The principal, on the other hand, has indicated to us that the doors were never locked and we seemed to have a contradiction in terms there."

"Okay."

"Are you able to resolve that for us?"

"Well, I can only tell you what the division's policy is."

"Okay."

"And the division's policy is that they not be locked."

"Fair enough, Sir."

"And this is an issue that has come up certainly in the past and it's very explicitly
the division's policy to not be locked."

Dave continued, "My understanding is that an incident like

this rocks a school division and a particular school. It's very stressful and very difficult. It affects all of the children; is that fair?"

"Oh, yes," Wiens said, "and continues to. I've been -- if I might add a little bit. I've been teaching for thirty-two years and this is probably one of the most difficult moments. This was one of the most difficult moments in those thirty-two years.

Dave continued, "And it's my understanding that a meeting took place between the children who were at the scene and who survived and the principal, Ms. Paul, a short time after the incident wherein she laid blame on those particular children. Did you take steps thereafter to remedy that situation and to assist those children in coping with what had happened?"

"Well, I'm not sure that I can respond to the kind of implication in terms of laying blame because I certainly would have heard that only secondhand." The parents did complain to Weins about the meeting.

"That would be hearsay. But I can respond to the part about taking steps. Certainly, most people know that one of the student's parents works in the office as secretary-treasurer. I went to the family home and met with them and indicated that I thought that he had acted -I'm talking about Gary Johns - had acted, you know, very bravely under the circumstances. But even before I was involved, we would have -- we had a crisis response team. And I should explain why I wasn't involved. I was home sick in bed when I got the call. We had a crisis response team in the school. They were there before I got there and they remained -- members of that team remained in the school for the remainder of the week and are still monitoring some of the students who are experiencing difficulty."

"My understanding is that although you've heard the information secondhand, you took it upon yourself to speak to Linda Paul about this particular meeting she had had with the children; is that right?"

"I have spoken to her."

"And you dealt with the matter internally?"

"Well, whatever "dealt with" means, yes."

"That's fine. To be fair to you, Sir, until yesterday, you had no idea that this particular piece of pipe that's been referred to as the culvert was installed on a contract basis for your school division; is that right?"

"No, I -- actually, it wasn't until this morning that I knew for sure, but it was raised -- the question was raised as to whether it would -- it had been installed under our auspices and I checked that out yesterday and, yes, it was. It was installed by an engineering firm which was engaged by our consultant. The engineering firm is S.E.G. Incorporated -- Engineers Incorporated and the -- our consultant is Lombard North."

"Is it your intention, as superintendent, to ensure that for any new facilities all possible safety measures are taken in the event there are drainage sites nearby such as this one?"

"Well, for certain we would be alert to this now. We knew beforehand that we had been involved in the -- with the City in looking after the drainage plan for that area, you know, in putting in place the drainage plan for that area. So I knew that. I was superintendent at the time. I was well aware that we had to provide -- because of our agreement with the City, we had to provide a plan which meant their -- met their specifications and was inspected by them regularly."

Dave asked, "And then the management of it afterwards, once it had been inspected in terms of the cleaning and maintenance, et cetera, did not fall on the school division but your understanding is that fell on the City of Winnipeg?"

"Well, that's -- it is not our property and it is my understanding that it is the City's responsibility, yes."

"And just on that photograph in front of you, can you tell us whether or not the roadway that leads into the teacher's parking lot is the property of the school or school division or the property of the City?"

"This is actually a very -- there's something extremely uncertain about whose property this is. I believe that it's our property. The -- and I'm not sure whether the -- but I'm not sure whether it's our property or the City's property. We have always treated it as our property. And that is true for this area west of the roadway as well, but we have an agreement with the City which I would have to check in terms of the swapping of the land and the joint use agreement of some of the land in this area because we own eleven - approximately eleven acres in that area."

"Thank you very much, Sir. Those are my questions."

20

"Step into the witness box. Do you wish to swear on the Bible or to be affirmed?" The court clerk was addressing the next witness.

"Bible," he said

"Would you place your right hand on the Bible and state your name to the Court."

"William Daniel Carroll."

Kelly was the first to question Carroll. "Mr. Carroll, my understanding is you are the Commissioner from Works and Operations?"

"That's correct."

"And briefly," Kelly asked, "what does that entail?"

"My responsibilities are to oversee the operations of the Water and Waste Department, the Hydro Electric System, the Streets and Transportation Department and the Transit System."

"So ultimately, for example, Mr. Pearson here would be reporting to yourself?"

"Through his director, yes."

"Through his director. Okay. It's obvious you're under subpoena with respect to the incident that occurred on April 22nd involving Mr. Adam Young? I understand from testimony that's occurred earlier today and yesterday that a report has been commissioned or consultants were retained by the City to not only look at the incident with Mr. Adam Young but also the overall situation with respect to culverts here in the City of Winnipeg?"

Carroll replied, "That's correct."

"Now, there has been some conflicting information provided," Kelly stated, "with respect to the status of that report. Can you update or can you inform the Court as to whether or not: a) such a report exists or at what stage it's at?"

"At this point in time, the consultants have been commissioned. That was authorized by the Board of Commissioners in July sometime, I think the 24th. They are out there doing their work. There's been no report drafted at this point in time. I believe our direction to the consultant has been to, instead of directing your efforts at writing the report down, do the work that you have to do in the field, attend to solving the problem in the field and produce the documentation later. So as far as I'm aware, there is no report at this stage of the game."

Finally, others could hear what I was hearing all along.. A look of confusion appeared on most of the faces in the gallery. In two days, we've heard that this mystery was ordered after the accident, in May, in mid June, after the inquest was called and now we're hearing July 25.

Something else struck me. When Bill Carroll mentioned that this report was authorized in July, how was it authorized. From my experience at City Hall, I knew nothing gets approved unless the Board of Commissioner's receives a report. Where is this report? Why wasn't it included in the evidence sent to the Crown?

Kelly went on. "So when there's talk of the draft report, that wouldn't exist, would it?"

"There's no draft report that I'm aware of," Carroll stated.

"Okay. And with respect to quotes that have been circulated through the press with respect to the final report being completed, of course that would be inaccurate?"

"There is no final report."

"Are you personally involved in following up on this report and ensuring it's done."

"Well, in the end the responsibility will come to me to ensure that the report is done and is tabled at the proper forums."

"So at this point you're not playing a direct role with respect to that report?"

"No, I'm not."

"I have no other questions for the commissioner." Kelly sat at his table.

After Judge Guy addressed Dave, he stood and turned to Carroll. "Commissioner Carroll, do you have a copy of the Works and Operations' report of investigation on this whole matter?"

"A copy of the Works and Operations' report?"

"Yes."

"There is no Works and Operations' report."

"There is no Works and Operations' report? Have you been provided with any report other than those from the fire department and the City of Winnipeg Police Service in regard to this matter?"

"I have a report from the department on this matter. That report was not tabled at the Works and Operations Committee."

"Which department, Sir?"

"Water and Waste Department."

"Do you have a copy of that report with you?"

"No, I do not."

"Were you asked to bring with you any documents relative to this matter?"

"No, I was not."

Another report that was not turned over.

"Are you conversant at all with the problem itself with culverts or are you more concerned about the administrative aspects of implementing a solution?"

"I guess by the nature of my job, I'm more concerned with sort of the higher level issues surrounding the culverts."

"Were you advised at any point in May or June that there were insufficient resources to do the job in remedying this dangerous situation?"

"I guess that by the nature of the fact that we hired consulting engineers to assist us then, obviously, we at that time decided we needed outside help to deal with it."

"Have you been informed or are you aware of what work has been completed to date in terms of remedying this situation?"

"The last I was told there were 70 installations of the 175 that were identified that have been completed and the plan was to complete the rest, 146 or something, by the time the snow is on the ground."

Dave asked, "And that information came to you how recently, Sir?"

"Within the last two weeks."

"Fair enough. "

"I shared that information with the standing committee."

"Are you aware of any studies having been done prior to the death of Adam Young as to the water flow in this particular area in the sewers and the drainage system?

"No, I am not."

"And, of course," Dave asked, "if such reports had been done they would have been forwarded to you?"

"Not necessarily," Carroll said. "Normally, the reports that sort of flow up to my level are reports that require policy decision, reports that require forwarding onto a standing committee for financial reasons or other reasons. So there are many reports created in the organization at a lower level that deal with all kinds of detail that I don't ever see.

"Can you tell us any reason why Mr. Young and his family were denied access to the reports that they requested back in the spring and early summer?"

"To the best of my knowledge, they were given all of the information that they requested. So I can't answer beyond that."

Dave started to ask, "So you're not aware of --"

"Unless there was some substantive reason that they couldn't be given this information."

"You're not aware of them being denied access to particular reports?"

"No."

"Okay. Do you have any explanation for why my friend, Mr. Moar, had difficulty obtaining the entire police report?"

"On the police report issue, I've seen the documentation from the police that said that there was two files and these files were not merged together properly and one file was sent and one file wasn't. That's the story as far, as I know. I have no reason to believe that that isn't the case."

"Those are my questions, Sir."

Judge guy asked, "Any questions, Mr. Samphir?"

"No, Your Honour," Samphir replied.

"Thank you, Mr. Carroll. You're excused. You can go.

Thank you," Guy replied.

"With respect, Your Honour," Kelly said, "those are the witnesses that the Crown intends to call. There were other witnesses subpoenaed that I discussed with my friends prior that subsequently were cancelled. That leaves the sole remaining issue whether Mr. Young again wants to address the Court.

Judge Guy looked at Dave, "Do you wish to make any comments, Mr. Guttman?"

"Thank you, Your Honour, Dave stood. "On behalf of Mr. Young and his family, first we would like to thank Mr. Moar for all of his diligence in regard to this matter. We would like to thank Your Honour for allowing us standing and the opportunity to ask questions over the last two days."

Dave went on, "I can indicate the biggest concern of the family is that this tragedy not reoccur. We're grateful and gratified to learn that the City has taken some measures. Mr. Young and his family, however, are mistrustful of promises from the City, information from the City, and I think, under all the circumstances, Your Honour can understand why."

"Therefore, we feel the need for Your Honour to study this matter and make very strong recommendations, particularly in regard to an inspection procedure for all of these sites, continued diligence in identifying any potential hazardous sites, and most importantly to formulate a policy that will ensure that a site like this cannot be erected again without proper safeguards. It seems to me incomprehensible that over the last five and a half months there hasn't been a policy formulated. There's been talk of one from the department level; there's talk about a consultant; there's talk about recommendations that will come in a final report, but Mr. Young and his family haven't seen anything."

"The spring run-off is not that far away, it's only a few months away and it would be tragic if anything remotely resembling this incident happened again. In fact, it would almost border on criminal negligence in our view, Your Honour. This situation must be corrected and any recurrence must be prevented."

"We leave it to Your Honour to make the appropriate recommendations in that regard."

Dave continued, "With respect to the school division, we have concerns about supervision. Certainly, the cost of education has grown rapidly since some of us were students in primary, elementary school and junior high school, but nonetheless children require supervision."

"We urge you to consider advising and recommending to the Department of Education that their policies be reviewed and, if necessary, utilize the resources of parents as volunteers to supervise the children outside of the school building itself immediately before classes, immediately after classes, and over the lunch hour. It shouldn't take a tragedy like this for people to begin to wonder who looks after my kids when they are outside of the classroom or outside of the lunchroom, but I think all of us are wondering, any of us that have children in school, what might happen. It shouldn't necessarily involve culverts; it can involve any type of thing that's adjacent to a school or on the school property. We think that that's very important."

In summary, Your Honour," Dave said, "the Young family feels that it's important that everybody recognize the tragedy they have suffered, but it's more important that Adam's death mean something and unless some serious changes take place with regard to these drainage systems, his death won't have meant anything and that would be another tragedy in and of itself."

"Those are my comments, Your Honour. Thank you."

"Any comments you wish to make, Mr. Samphir?" Guy asked.

"No, Your Honour, no comments," Samphir replied. He was smiling again.

"Well, I think I want to thank Counsel for their assistance in this matter and I'm -- and I think I can speak for all of us: we obviously want to do everything we can to prevent a reoccurrence of this kind of tragedy from happening, Guy said as he addressed the court room. "That's the purpose of the inquest and hopefully that will be the -- what can happen as a result. Thank you."

21

It's the day after the inquest. October 16, 1997. The Salvation Army and the Fire Department had planned to dedicate an evergreen tree in honour of Adam. The tree was planted in front of the fire hall on Leila, about 30 feet from where Adam died.

Friends, family and Adam's classmates all gathered in the fire hall. The school band played one of Adam's favorite songs. Fire Chief Barry Lough said a few words, as did Mike O'Shaughnessy. Only Mike cried at the end of his.

We planned to present to the firemen, an award. We wanted to let them know how much their efforts were appreciated. During the presentation, I was overcome with emotion and couldn't finish the speech the I had planned. It was too much. The inquest was still fresh, plus today was my birthday.

After the formal proceedings inside the hall, Captain Lewis asked everyone to tie a white ribbon around the tree. Everyone took their turn tying and after, Michelle tied a big ribbon on top. It's still their today.

Kevin, Marc, Jake and Aaron released a bunch of helium balloons in the air. As the balloons floated up, the crowd of almost 100 people remained silent. The balloons floated up over the fire hall and the wind took them over the school.

Once over the school, they seemed to stop. They hung there for a moment and then disappeared over the horizon.

As the balloons disappeared, the crowd dispersed back inside the fire hall.

People mingled, drinking coffee. I stood outside by myself.

Mike walked over and handed me a cigarette.

"I'm glad you came," I said.

"Hey, I wouldn't miss this. I don't care what the legal department said," he said. "What do they have to do with this?" I asked.

"There was a couple of us invited, but the lawyers didn't think it was appropriate for any of us to come. I told them where to go."

I was tired. Tired of fighting. The inquest was over. There were still questions left unanswered. The culverts still weren't fixed. I felt like all this was for nothing.

One of Adam's friend's mother approached me as I walked back into the hall. "Adam used to be at our place a lot, she said. "He talked about you all the time. I wish my son had the same relationship with his father. He used to say you were his hero, he wanted to be just like you, and now I can see why."

October 16, 1997. My birthday. I had just been given the best birthday gift ever.

22

"Rob, we've got a problem. Someone trying to set you up." It was Dave on the phone. 9:30 at night. The night before I was supposed to go on Peter Warren's show.

"Someone from the City has sent a copy of a letter to the media and their trying set you up. They know you're going on Warren's show in the morning and he could slam you," he said.

"What's in this letter? Who's it from?" I asked.

"Bill Carroll wrote it and sent it to the Mayor and all the City Councillor's. Someone from the legal department faxed it to the media. I'll get you a copy of it," he said.

I called the Free Press. Yes, they received a copy of the letter. The reporter wanted my comments. I told him I hadn't seen it. He faxed me a copy.

I couldn't believe it. Here was a four page letter to the Mayor and City Council explaining everything. It was dated October 17, two days after the inquest and it was written by Bill Carroll, the man who at the inquest claimed to not know any details.

The letter explained what happened on the day Adam died. How he was swept into a culvert which drains into the land drainage sewer. Carroll wrote that the City would undertake all things necessary to prevent further tragedies. He went on to say what wonderful things the City had done immediately after the accident. Like on June 23, they fixed all the culverts.

FOR MY SON

Carroll wrote how the installation was done without the City's authorization but, that the City inspected and approved the final result.

The letter went on to say how many culverts the City found and how many were fixed. The $200,000 UMA Engineering report was close to being completed.

The last page of the letter was about me. He claimed that I was never denied access to information. Basically discrediting everything I had said and done.

The top of the letter showed where it was faxed from. The City of Winnipeg Legal Services.

I paced in the lobby of CJOB the next morning, waiting for Peter Warren to escort me into the studio. Dave had strongly suggested that I cancel the interview. No! I had nothing to hide.

When I entered the studio, I saw Warren had the letter in front of him.

"Did you see this?" he asked.

"Yes."

"What do you think," he said.

"Well, if you read it carefully, you'll see the holes," I said. "First of all, Bill Carroll claimed, at the inquest to not know much about the entire incident, yet one day later he writes a five page explanation of everything. He goes on to say the $200,000 consultants report was ordered in anticipation of litigation, not for remedial measures. And then he goes on to say that I wasn't denied access to information. If that's the case, why did they send me these letters."

I pulled the denial letters out of my file and handed them to Peter. He read them then looked at me. "I know this letter from Carroll is crap. I just wanted to see what your reaction was going to be," he said.

"You have to be careful," he said. They are going to do anything they can to discredit you, make you look like the grieving father that doesn't know what he's saying or doing. I've seen it before."

"They can do and say what they want," I said. "I think I've got the support behind me."

"I need to ask you something," Peter aid. He pulled a page of the Winnipeg Sun out of his file. Above the article, was picture of Michelle, Dave and I walking out of the Law Courts Building. He pointed to Michelle. "Who's this?" he asked.

"That's Michelle. My girlfriend. Why?"

"On my voice mail this morning, there was two messages asking why Adam's mother wasn't around. The City's going to try and use this. They're searching for anything they can to get you. You've hurt them pretty bad. If it comes up this morning, you should be prepared," he said.

"Kim's been in bad shape ever since the accident. She hasn't read a newspaper, listened to the radio or watched the news. She couldn't handle this. I can. There's not much more they can do to me."

"Okay. That's fine. I'm just saying be careful."

23

In early November the City Legal Department finally agreed to meet with Dave and I. Judge Guy's report from the inquest had not been completed and I think they hoped to resolve this before it was released. Marvin Samphir's first comment set the stage.

Seated next to another city lawyer, Marvin opened with, "It's obvious from the inquest that we have nothing to do with this. There's no liability on our part."

Dave replied, "Well, I think your mistaken. All you have to do read the transcripts. It say's it all right there."

"I think your mistaken," Marvin said. "Any comments prior to Judge Guy's report would be premature."

Dave and Marvin continued with their conversation. Several areas were discussed, but nothing of significance.

Until the issue of the missing reports.

"Your client has seen everything there is," Marvin said. "All the reports were given to the Crown prior to the inquest.

"What about the Works and Operations report?" Dave asked.

"There isn't one. There never was," Marvin replied.

"The Water and Waste report?"

"There isn't one."

"Why did Bill Carroll mention a Water and Waste report at the inquest?" Dave asked.

Marvin replied, " I don't know. It's just a coincidence."

I'd had enough. I looked at Marvin and asked, "Where's the report that went to the Board of Commissioners requesting the $200,000 for the engineers?"

Marvin was stunned.

He turned to Kim Carswell, then to me. "How did you know about that one?"

"I know that whenever that amount of money is spent, it's a decision of the Board, and they won't make a decision unless there's a report."

"You forget, Marvin," Dave said, "my client used to work here. He knows exactly how this place runs."

Marvin looked at me. "You'll never see that report. We'll bury it. We'll claim privilege."

At that point we agreed to disagee. Marvin asked Dave to provide him with examples of cases to prove that they were liable.

The next five months were the same. Nothing much had happened. There was promises of an offer of settlement from the City's legal department, but those never materialized. Letters and phone calls would go days with a response. Reports never did turn up, even though they were always two weeks away from being finalized.

There were threats from the legal department to Dave. "If your client continues to talk to the media, we have a plan B we can use against him," was one of them.

Two hours after the official lawsuit was filed, members of the media received anonymous phone calls saying I had signed a huge book deal to profit from my son's death. Fortunately, the journalists that received these calls had become friends and knew the comments weren't true. They knew what was going on.

In December of 1997, Judge Guy released his report from the inquest. His recommendations were almost identical to our conditions of the settlement. He made four recommendations in total. He wanted all the sites inspected and corrective action taken, new policies were to be in place, reports made public and that the City should continue to identify any potentially hazardous sites.

Guy's final comments were interesting. He wrote "a citizen of the City would assume that inherent in any inspection as to standards would include a safety factor. To limit the inspection as to what might be described as only economical factors regarding easier inventory purchasing and life expectancy might be viewed too narrow even in light of the design professional's safety responsibility."

"The public might assume that if the City is going to inspect because of their responsibility in this field then it should be for all purposes and they should not rely on the design professional's responsibility."

In other words, the City is us. The politicians, the bureaucrats, the legal department and the engineers should be working for us. In our best interests. They are public servants, and we are the public.

After Adam died, the professionals should have met to address remedial measures, to prevent another tragedy, to stop another child from dying.

Instead the legal department met to discuss ways to limit their liability, to find ways to cover themselves from the responsibility.

In my opinion, these public servants served themselves. They took a child's death, a father's plea, and a Court of Queen's Bench Judge's recommendations under advisement. No actions, just reactions. And reactions for all the wrong reasons.

They did not serve the public. They didn't serve me and certainly they didn't serve Adam, my son.

24

It's now been almost a year since Adam died, and seven months since the inquest. I'm sitting at the kitchen table talking to Leslie McLaren, a reporter from CBC Radio. She wanted to talk about how things were going now that it was coming up to the one year anniversary of the accident.

She also wanted to get my comments about Tom Pearson doing an interview later that afternoon, basically saying that the City had fixed all the dangerous culverts and to say what a wonderful job they had done throughout this tragedy.

"Tom Pearson says they've fixed all 243 culverts. What's your opinion of that?" she asked.

"That's great that they fixed all those, but what about the rest," I said. "Last year they claimed to have lost their records so they didn't know where these installations were. How can they say they've fixed them all."

"Do you know of any others that aren't fixed?" she asked.

We went for a drive. No more than mile. We found three.

"Is it over, Rob?" Leslie asked.

"No," I said after thinking for a minute.

How can it be over. I've lost a son and a career. I've lost a year of my life and nothing's changed. Culverts are still open. Kevin tells me the school doors are still locked at lunch time. I still miss Adam. There are some days I can't get out of bed in the morning. There are days when I want to run away. What's changed.

I tried to fight the system. Some people say I won. The City has made us an offer of settlement. One of our conditions of settlement is to see the reports. They can't seem to find them.

Judge Guy's recommendations were taken under advisement. That's it.

Taken under advisement.

Dear Adam

Just thought I'd let know how what's been happening since you've gone.

I don't work at City Hall anymore. I don't even talk to very many people there.

I've started a new job and thing seem to be going well.

Kevin and Marc are doing fine. Kevin goes to a different school now. He seemed to have a lot of trouble concentrating and getting things done at your old school. It doesn't surprise me. All your friends transferred to other schools too.

Kevin seems to like his new school, at least that's what he tells me. He doesn't seem to talk very much. Sometimes I'll see him staring off, looking at nothing. When I ask him what's wrong, he says "nothing".

Marc's still the same. Getting into trouble as usual. He seems to want to spend a lot more time with me and that's nice.

FOR MY SON

Last Christmas I woke up at three o'clock in the morning, I heard something. I found Marc crying in the living. He had plugged in the Christmas lights and was sitting in front of the tree. I sat down beside him and he said, "Sometimes Adam used to be a real pain. But I sure miss him."

We all miss you, Squirt. Everyday it always seems like something is missing.

Remember the Mustang we were rebuilding. I never had the chance to tell you, but that was going to be your birthday present when you turned sixteen. I stopped working on it. To tell you the truth, I don't even know where it is and I don't want to. It doesn't seem worth it.

I'm not fighting with the City anymore. I think everything is finished. It was hard. I lost most of my friends there and I got fired.

Sometimes I felt that if I fought hard, kept to my beliefs, and won, maybe it would bring you back. It didn't work. I do know though, that no one else will ever go the way you did. You and I made sure of that, didn't we.

I saw one of your friend's mom the other day. She says you said I was your hero and you always wanted to be like me. I hope you still feel the same way. I always wanted you to be proud of me. I know I'm proud of you and I always will be.

I sure miss you and hope to see you soon. Take care and keep watching over us.

Love Dad